I0691251

Six Keys

Sue L. Clarke

Grosvenor House
Publishing Limited

This book is published by
Grosvenor House Publishing Ltd
Link House
140 The Broadway, Tolworth, Surrey, KT6 7HT.
www.grosvenorhousepublishing.co.uk

A CIP record for this book
is available from the British Library

ISBN 978-1-80381-567-1

In memory of my dad, Terry Clarke

1

Chapter

Chadwick was in a foul mood. It was the second time he had failed to make partner. His name would remain third in the legal trinity of Fortescue, Bright and Chadwick. Even the halo of ginger hair sat disappointedly on the edge of his gleaming forehead. Bright didn't deserve the honour and now Chadwick would be stuck with even more meetings like this; a will reading and a messy one at that.

'If you could all take a seat, this really won't take a moment. Have you had your ID checked and received your passes?' he paused. 'Well? Have you? No of course you haven't. Veronica!' Chadwick was in no mood to be trifled with. 'Take them downstairs! Yes all of them. I won't ask why they weren't checked in. I won't even ask why they have no clearance or passes. But I will ask why *you* didn't ask!' Veronica winced, we all did.

'If you could just follow me.' she said rather shakily.

Our group didn't get as far as the lift. Brown simply appeared as if out of nowhere. He gave us each an ID pass, switched off his mobile phone and then peered over his glasses, looking at each one of us.

1

'What the fuck is Brown doing here? It was bad enough that he attended the funeral. It's like some weird Agatha Christie film and as for that...'

'Hush Shauna. Let's go and find out what Barry has left us all in his will.' A useful deflection from Andy. He had been chosen as Shauna's behaviour monitor, not an easy task with one so volatile. Our group needed to find things out, not close things down.

'That was fast.' Chadwick said somewhat disappointedly. 'Please be seated and...'

'Not meaning to interrupt...'

'But interrupting all the same. And if you could introduce yourself. I was expecting five clients.'

'Indeed. It is a little delicate. Perhaps we could step outside for a moment.'

'Are you named in the will?'

'I believe so.'

Then ask one of these lovely ladies to shuffle along and take a seat.'

'I'd rather stand.' Chadwick unsuccessfully disguised a sneer.

'As you wish. No interrupting. That goes for everyone. State your full names for the record. Veronica! Is this recording?' Veronica hastily checked the recorder and nodded nervously at Mr Chadwick, her eyes averted from his beady headlights.

Our group introduced themselves, here was a team that had quite literally been thrown together: Welsh Andy (42) the conman and the comedian, Brian (37) the social worker, straight-laced and serious, Shauna (29) the youth worker and the mouthpiece, Berni (62) the psychic and caregiver and myself, Helena (57) the

2

teacher and thinker/worrier. Chadwick was suitably unimpressed and his voice soon dropped to a dull monotone and he droned on for some time. Andy was chewing mindlessly on a yellow Bic Biro, Berni was fixed in position, her crossed arms providing a suitable prop to support her, Brian's restless leg disorder had kicked in and his heel pounded the floor like a pneumatic drill. Shauna began searching for her 'emergency mints', a clear indicator that her patience was waning and I was thinking about Barry. Six weeks had now passed since his death and as the saying goes when one door closes, another door shuts in your face. The circumstances surrounding Barry's death were still unclear and unanswered questions hung limply in the air. But Barry had not quite finished toying with us yet. Even now, when Barry was dead and gone, he'd never really gone.

Fortunately, Chadwick's voice appeared to be tailing off. Never one to disappoint, he jolted us into the present.

'That's the legal claptrap over with, now a message from your colleague or friend, either or.'

Chadwick had a home he'd rather go to, or more likely a pub he'd rather be drinking in. He bristled like a wire brush, his hamster brown eyes dulled, unable to emit any token of warmth.

Barry had left detailed written instruction in his will. We had not been left anything individually, just an envelope addressed to us collectively as 'The Watchers' with our names listed below. Brown smiled smugly when he received his own personally addressed envelope.

3

'You are hereby advised to open and read these letters here at Fortescue, Bright and Chadwick. This is at the client's request. A private room for both parties is to be provided if required.' Chadwick read the message with the same enthusiasm as one would read back their weekly shopping list for Asda. Chadwick stood up abruptly. He couldn't resist one last blast at Veronica.

'Of course you need to ask them all to sign the receipts! How old are you, ten?'

I could feel that Shauna was champing at the bit. Brian had managed to ram his foot against the leg of her chair to prevent an uprising and keep her penned in at the table.

We all dutifully signed the receipts. Shauna threw the pen across the table carelessly and it landed just by me.

'Just leave it Helena, who gives a …'

'Thank you Shauna, I have it.' I said whilst placing the pen back on the table in front of Chadwick and throwing her a warning glance.

Brown wanted a private room. It was easier for us to stay where we were and focus at keeping Shauna under control. What was there to hide? Was this just another weird, attention seeking game that Barry was taunting us with? Brown was escorted away by Veronica who was still keen to make amends.

'I'll leave the room for a short break whilst you confer.' Chadwick said as he creaked to his feet and straightened his maroon silk tie.'

'What a load of …'

'Shall I do the honours?' Brian skilfully interrupted Shauna.

'Go ahead. What a crazy bastard Barry turned out to be, even in death.'

4

'Let's not be too harsh. We have no idea what this letter is going to say.'

'I couldn't give a …'

This time Shauna was interrupted by the sound of a key as it fell onto the glass desk and then the tiled floor. It was a big key.

'That, is a safety deposit box key.' Andy said, as he retrieved it and placed it on the table.

'What else is in the envelope?' Berni asked gently.

Brian pulled out a piece of stiff blue paper, Basildon Bond no doubt, knowing Barry. And then just in the distance, just at the very edge of hearing, I thought I could hear a song. Convinced my mind was playing tricks on me and that Flint, aka Alan Rickman, wouldn't dare toy with one of my favourite showmen and songwriters. I shook my head. Flint had no shame.

One Voice

Barry Manilow

It takes that one voice
Just one voice, singing in the darkness
All it takes is one voice
Shout it out and let it ring
Just one voice, it takes that one voice
And everyone will sing

2

Chapter

The visit to Fortescue, Bright and Chadwick Solicitors had successfully dispelled any doubts. Barry was dead, really dead. Not sedated or trapped in a *Watcher 22* flashback, quite simply dead. Whether Barry was the new or the old version of his original self, matters not. The secrets may have died with him. The light in Barry's eyes really did go out just two weeks after the party, at the end of July. There would be no more group hugs for Barry. He was one of the originals and for all his faults, I would truly miss him. The medical report seemed straight forward enough, it wasn't the cause of death that was the problem, it was the timing. A heart attack can strike whenever it pleases, but the chances of it coinciding with a major time travelling incident, with Barry at centre stage, was another story. Over the past few months we had only managed to scratch away at the top layer of secrecy which shielded both the large corporations and MI5. There were many unanswered questions and no real possibility of ever getting the answers, well not using conventional methods.

There was no theme to Barry's wake, no dressing up or Abba songs. We'd had a group meeting, using face time,

6

to discuss our approach. Shauna was unsurprisingly very loud, her anger spilling out unedited. She voiced the scepticism we all felt about the timing of Barry's heart attack. Andy was more philosophical and Berni, as you would expect, was quiet and reflective. Brian was the more practical member of the group and dealt with the planning and logistics. As for me, I was still coming to terms with his death. We had been through such a lot together and sadness seeped through me as memories flooded back. There had been no official word from XP, the company who designed and ran the *Watcher 22* programme. But at the funeral, a garland of black poppies was discreetly laid at the graveside by a man clad in a trademark navy suit. He was wearing sunglasses despite the barrage of clouds that sprawled across the British summer sky.

The wake was predictably dreadful, until the alcohol kicked in. Barry's wife had died long since, before they'd had a chance to start a family. Some distant relatives of Barry's attended and at times I felt that I saw a glimmer of him flicker in their eyes, but this may have been exacerbated by the large glass of Jack Daniels that Andy had poured for me on my arrival. There were a few pinstripes, with their corporate wives in tow, they looked bored and were itching to leave. This was a sad little group, a mish-mash of worlds that seemed to represent the disparity in Barry's life and the uncertainty which encompassed his death.

I managed to glance across at Berni, her eyes were not brimming with tears as I'd expected, she just seemed sad and distracted. Shauna was her usual self, an untamed force of nature, ready to launch into orbit with only the slightest provocation. As always, Brian was the calming influence. It was all going as smoothly as these things can and then Andy touched my elbow and turned me gently towards the door.

'Say nothing Helena. Just watch will you?' the Welsh lilt in his voice was just noticeable. I squinted hard to see outside into the sunlight, the whisky not assisting with focus. And this was the first time I saw him. Dressed in a black overcoat and those patent black shoes which catch the sunlight, he at least had the courtesy to stand at a discrete distance. It was Brown.

'I think we need to get gobby out of here before she sets eyes on Brown.' Andy said as quietly as he could. 'No need to create a scene and Brown probably only knows as much as we do.'

'I'll speak to Berni, she looks like she's ready to leave and perhaps she'll bring the car around and we can guide our flock out of here.'

'Are you taking the piss Helena with one of your Welshy inferences?'

'What? No…. is this because I mentioned the word flock? Jesus Andy, only mild paranoia.'

Berni moved swiftly, sensing an imminent altercation. She looked over towards me and made the internationally recognised sign for leaving, indicating her head towards the door. I nodded in confirmation. Minutes later she returned with her sleek Jaguar which she gently pulled up to the doorway, blocking Brown out of the picture. We all piled in, grateful to be leaving. An unusual silence fell in the car and then on the very edge of hearing, a faint tune drifted into the air, muffled by the car engine. I said nothing, hoping that no one else could hear it.

'What the fuck's that noise?' said Shauna whilst shooting me a knowing look.

'Yes what is that noise Helena?' Brian asked gently.

'I don't see why I should know, just because....'

'Just because *you're* the only one with the psycho Guide, who can still seem to taunt us with his warped record collection. That's why.'

'I haven't heard from Flint in a long time, you all know that.'

Silence fell again. Berni caught my eye in the mirror and then raised her eyebrows, asking the question without words. I lay my head back on the smooth leather seat and the combination of Jack Daniels and the movement of the car led me to close my eyes. My thoughts drifted. They say that hearing is the last thing to leave you when you are dying and perhaps it's the same with sleeping, as now I could definitely hear it. There was only one person tactless enough to be playing this at Barry's wake, it had to be Flint.

Paint It, Black

The Rolling Stones

I see a line of cars and they're all painted black
With flowers and my love, both never to come back

3

Chapter

The wake was over. I shuddered and brought myself back to the reality of the day. The jangle of the key, as it hit the tiles, helped to bring me back to the present and Chadwick's office.

'Shall I?'

'Yes, get on with it Brian for fuck's sake, before the 'Brown noser' gets back.' Shauna said, clearly agitated. I could hear Andy, chuckling to himself.

'Brown noser... that's brilliant...'

'Brian and Shauna, control yourselves. It's not pantomime season. Could we please hear the words of our dear friend Barry on this sombre occasion...' Berni interrupted.

Brian coughed and took a deep breath. All eyes were focused on him.

'Dearly beloved... just a joke my friends. These are Barry's words not mine.' Brian added anxiously. 'Obviously you are reading this following my demise and by now you will be wondering what the safety deposit key will reveal. Sadly it's not a cache of diamonds or details to a secret offshore account containing millions. Patience my dear friends, I know that you all have questions. I would like to assure each and every one of you that I am and always was the same Barry that you knew and were hopefully fond of. It's safer for everyone if I don't commit any more to paper, I am hoping that the clues I give you will lead us all to the answers that I know we are all seeking. Sadly, there are others on the same trail from less salubrious backgrounds. I ask you to act with caution and take great care, especially when visiting the bank. I suggest you go into the bank in pairs with the other members of the team posted as look-outs. These are dangerous times my friends and I, by all accounts, am now deceased. Use all the skills that you have learnt, you are stronger in numbers, keep a tight-knit group and don't hesitate in calling upon Cagney and Lacey (Special Forces) should you need to, they have been briefed. Brown will be your contact with the authorities, but he is under strict instructions to lay low. Lastly, I just want to assure you all that I loved being a part of our very special group and it saddens me to know that I lost your trust. I hope that the keys and clues will be enough to guide you and provide us all with some sense of closure. Please burn this after reading. I kid you not. Chadwick will dispose of all the evidence. With the kindest of regards, Barry.'

'Bleedin' hell. Why didn't he just tell us if he's the Barry we know or the younger version?'

'Because Shauna it would place us all in great danger, you should realise that by now.' Berni said quietly.

'Yeah well, It's all a bit fuckin' far-fetched if you ask me?'

'Lucky that we didn't then.' Andy was losing patience.

The door clicked open and Chadwick entered the room. He emitted a small sigh, which was duly accompanied by the creak of an equally tired spring in his faded leather backed chair.

'All done? Kindly pass me the letter Brian and I will shred it immediately as instructed.... and before you say anything Shauna the shredded material is incinerated and not reconstructed by Tom Cruise. This isn't a version of *Mission Impossible*.'

Brown tapped politely on the door. Chadwick inclined his head towards me, indicating that I was to let him into the room. I gave him a powerful glare and a raise of the eyebrow, before opening the door. Brown gave a conciliatory nod and Chadwick continued.

'As Executor of the will, I now provide you with a copy of the death certificate and an accompanying letter of confirmation. I must stress that you will also need proof of identity to ...' Chadwick paused, 'to deal with other confidential matters. Any further questions?'

'Yeah. I have one.' Shauna said in a dangerously quiet voice. 'Can you tell us any more about his death?'

Chadwick sighed. 'We await the coroner's report, as you would know if you'd read the correspondence.' This was a brave response to someone as volatile as Shauna.

The group collectively held their breath. Shauna raised the tempo.

'So Chadwick, am I right in thinkin' that it's your job to represent Barry? Yeah. So, is it too much to fuckin' ask that you do just that, without being so bleedin' patronising and also...' This time it was my turn to diffuse the situation.

'Well I think we've heard quite enough for now. Thank you Mr. Chadwick. We'll just be on our way.'

The group had taken the hint and grabbed coats and turned Shauna towards the door, ready for a quick exit.

'Delighted I'm sure.' Chadwick said somewhat foolishly. Shauna pushed back against Brian who was ready to square up to Chadwick. Berni and I forced the group forward and we exploded into the corridor like a cork popping out of a bottle. Fizzing and bubbling, we managed to get Shauna into the lift and then out of the building.

And this was only the beginning. I heard the very faintest of chuckles in the distance. I knew it was Flint once the music started.

Absolute Beginners

David Bowie

I've nothing much to offer
There's nothing much to take
I'm an absolute beginner
And I'm absolutely sane

4

Chapter

Exactly one week later, our team met again at a small cafe just opposite the bank. Meetings were always arranged face-to-face for security reasons. None of us trusted the conventional ways of keeping in touch. At each meeting, we planned the time and date of the next.

'Did everyone check that they weren't being followed?' Brian said cautiously, before sipping his flat white.

'Not as far as I could tell.' Andy said seriously.

'At least this area is pedestrianised, so we don't have to worry about being whisked off by a black BMW.' Berni added, smiling weakly. She looked tired. It was a long journey to Manchester for her. I patted her hand reassuringly.

'We're hiding in plain sight this time Berni.'

'What the fuck does that even mean?' Shauna said loudly, so much so that a mother grimaced and made a tutting sound as she turned the pram away from our table. 'As if a baby is going to understand the F word...'

'Shauna if we could just focus on today's mission and try to keep your voice down.'

'I agree with Helena, button it mouthy. We have bigger fish to fry.' Andy said pointedly.

Shauna scraped back her chair in annoyance. She noisily slurped her diet coke and ground the ice between

14

her teeth. It was always best to ignore her at times like these.

'Do we draw lots or ask for volunteers?'

'It's not a bank job Helena, we're not breaking out of Colditz. Anyhow, I've got a copy of the death certificate and the letter of confirmation that Chadwick gave us at the meeting. I have also brought my ID as instructed.' Andy paused. 'I'm putting myself forward for the first visit to the bank. I think it would be a good idea to go in pairs, one male and one female as it might be a bit less conspicuous.'

'I'm not arsed about going this time.' Shauna said loudly over her shoulder as she headed for the counter to purchase a piece of millionaire's shortbread.

'I'll go if you want Helena.' Berni said nervously. I could tell that she'd rather not. It was time to step up.

'It's OK Berni, I'll go with Andy. I have my ID.'

'Come on then Helena, let's crack on.' And without further ado, Andy and I left the cafe, nervously watching the people in the square.

'No one will stop us here Helena. Firstly it's too crowded and secondly, because it would be pointless, we haven't collected anything yet.'

'I agree with you Andy. I think we'll need our wits about us on the way out though.'

'I'm going to call Brian before we leave and get him to wait outside the bank and then we can meet Shauna and Berni as we arranged.'

'Good thinking. Here we go then.'

It just looked like a normal bank, about the size of a city centre branch, but nothing fancy. Andy politely held open the glass door for me and then we were in.

'I don't think that this is something you go in the normal queue for.' I whispered to Andy.

'I agree. Let's walk over to the Customer Service desk.' Andy grabbed my hand and we approached the desk together. I smiled weakly, this felt very uncomfortable. We gave a brief explanation and our letters and proof of ID were then photocopied by Jodie, a very helpful young Assistant. We were then asked to take a seat on the tangerine chairs and wait to be summoned. Jodie made a few phone calls and then nodded reassuringly, before calling us over.

'Frederick will take you down. Ah good, here he is. Hi Freddie, these are the customers, could you get them up to speed with the protocol? Lovely Thank you.' Jodie was quick to move on to the next customer as Freddie manoeuvred us toward his desk behind a tinted curved screen.

'Please.' he indicated for us to sit. He loved to swivel on his black leather chair. I guessed his age to be early thirties. I used to work in a bank and although I loathed it with every fibre of my being, I always loved the people.

'Have you opened a safety deposit box before?' Freddie asked, his body facing us but his eyes fixed on the computer screen. He seemed suitably unimpressed.

Andy filled him in and he seemed a little more interested.

'It sounds like something out of a film.' he said whilst smoothing the edges of a mousey brown moustache in a suitably Inspector Clouseau fashion. 'Only one of you can enter the private viewing room with me. I will take you to the box, check you can unlock it, and then leave. So which one of you is it to be?'

'I'll go.' Andy said firmly. 'Can my friend remain here?'

'Yes just take a seat in the customer waiting area.' Freddie said to me. 'Jodie I'm taking Mr… Faraday down. If you'd like to follow me.'

Andy nodded reassuringly as he stood up to follow Freddie. I moved to the waiting area.

'Give Brian a ring and get the team moving.' Andy said quickly. 'We may want to leave quickly.' Andy followed Freddie, who keyed in a security code before they went through the reinforced security door.

'All OK Helena?' Brian answered his phone immediately.

Hi Brian, yes stage one is completed, if you could begin the preparation for stage 2 that would be excellent. About ten minutes? Yeah sure.'

Jodie looked over at me and gave a weak smile. Perhaps my voice had been a little louder than I thought.

It had been half an hour. I could see the top of Brian's head through the window. He sent a text and I was just about to answer when Andy and Freddie emerged. Andy was carrying a brown notebook and envelope.

'Andy, let's stop for a moment. Shall I put those in my handbag or have you got zip pockets in your jacket?'

'We can't risk your handbag, Helena.' Andy said quietly. 'I'll put it in my inside pocket.' After making sure everything was securely zipped away, he looked out of the front window. 'Where is he, where's Brian?' he asked anxiously.

I could no longer see the top of Brian's head.

'You were quite a long time, maybe he needed the toilet.' We exited the bank and there was no sign of Brian.

'Shall I ring his phone?' I asked nervously.

'Let's go into one of the busy shops first, we're exposed here.' We hurried into the nearest chain store.

'I'll phone him.' Andy said abruptly as I pretended to look at the latest trends in outdoor wear, hiding a gasp at the price tag. 'There's no answer. We need to move and now!' Andy grabbed my hand and we made a speedy exit through a side door. And so it began. What had Barry got us into now?

I'm still standing

Elton John

You know I'm still standing better than I ever did
Looking like a true survivor, feeling like a little kid

5

Chapter

We were only slightly out of breath when we approached the rather majestic entrance of the Midland Hotel. It was originally built to serve the Manchester Central railway station, but today it would have a very different purpose. Andy tugged at my hand as we entered through one of the semi-circular archways, the gleaming brass door opened by an immaculately attired doorman.

'Where are we meeting them Helena?'

'Erm, the Octagon Bar.' I said distractedly as we moved across the lobby. The marvellous Art Deco columns and sweeping archways were lit by golden lamps.

'Come on, let's go in.' Andy said as he hurriedly pushed me through the doorway. We headed towards the reception area in too much of a rush to notice the recent refurbishments. As we dutifully took our place in the queue, a familiar voice shrieked our names. There was no mistaking Shauna's dulcet tones.

'Jesus Christ.' Andy muttered under his breath, before turning and giving her the shut-up signal. He grabbed my hand and we made our way over to the navy blue banquette, positioned beautifully next to a tree that was base lit. Such scenes of grandeur served only to emphasise the scale of a binary opposite. Shauna was perched awkwardly on the edge of her seat, clearly feeling out of place. Berni was sipping her flat white, disguising her angst perfectly.

'Where the fuck is Brian and what did the bank give you and…'

'Shauna if you could keep your voice down, perhaps we won't be glared at quite so much and be asked to leave.'

Shauna pursed her lips in clear annoyance. Tapping her red varnished nails on the glass table in protest. Berni took the lead.

'I've ordered tea and sandwiches for you all, as a treat.'

'It is fuckin' mint here Andy. The prices are a right rip off…'

'Shauna! Just wait. We must focus on Brian.' Berni said firmly. 'Andy and Helena, what have you heard?'

'He just disappeared. Simple as.'

'We tried to phone him from one of the shops, but there was no answer and well not meaning to go all Jason Bourne on you, but Andy and I felt we were being followed.'

'Fuckin' great!! And which of you two geniuses then decided to meet up with the rest of the group here?' Shauna was irrepressible.

'We went through Kendals, no one could track us in there. Speaking of which can everyone turn off their phones? I don't think we're quite at the stage of taking out sim cards and destroying them. 'Andy said firmly.

'So what's our next move?' I asked looking around our little group.

We were interrupted by the arrival of a beautiful tray of teapots, cups and dainty sandwiches. Once everyone

20

had served themselves, I just had to ask Berni again if she thought that Brian was in serious danger.

'I don't feel that he is in imminent danger, not physically at least. We know that they will contact us and ask for the envelope from the safety deposit box. That's what they're really after. Now we have to decide if we should open the envelope or if that would risk Brian's safety.'

'I think that we need to know exactly what we are up against and what this envelope contains.' Andy said, whilst rubbing his chin thoughtfully.

Before anyone else could comment a phone began to ring. We all looked at each other expectantly, but it soon became clear that the phone did not belong to anyone in the group. Andy signalled for silence and within seconds Shauna had dropped to her knees and was feeling along the rim of the table. A triumphant grin confirmed success and Shauna nodded at us, always eager to gain our approval. We glanced at each other, before signalling for her to go ahead.

'Who the fuck are you and where's Brian?' Shauna never struggled in projecting her voice. Andy put his head in his hands and Berni just sighed.

'Hang on a minute, slow down you toss....'

'Here's a pen Shauna.' Berni interrupted expertly. By this time we were receiving several hostile glares, which wasn't helped by Shauna scribbling the message down on one of the hotel's perfectly pressed linen serviettes.

'Yeah got it. Can I speak to Brian before you...he put the bleedin' phone down on me, the bastard...'

This was the final straw for the staff at the Midland Hotel who were, quite rightly, used to a more tranquil clientèle. Before the Head Waiter could get to our table, Andy bundled Shauna out through the lobby and we left tout suite.

We found a suitable seating area in the centre of a pedestrianised street. Not ideal but a respite from the glares and pressure of trying to keep Shauna under control.

'What did they say Shauna?' Berni asked gently. Shauna reached into her pocket and pulled out the napkin. 'All they said was that we've got to meet up outside the Town Hall at 4 o'clock and give them the envelope. Then we get Brian back. They didn't even use their real voices it was one of those voice changer apps, cowardly bastard, oh, and we must **not** contact the Police or MI5 or anyone else or the deal is off. And also that the woman who entered the bank, that's you Helena, will bring the envelope and await further instruction.'

'Now we have a very difficult decision to make. We have little time but we need to proceed very carefully.'

'We are goin' for Brian though, we all agree...'

'Yes, Shauna that's not what I mean.'

'I think that Berni is referring to the envelope, the one that Helena and I just picked up from the bank. The question is should we open it before trading it for Brian's life?'

'Is it sealed with one of those wax seals Andy or just a normal envelope seal?' Andy retrieved the envelope and examined it with great care.

'It's just a buff envelope, feels like there's just a letter inside and the seal is just one of those glued-down ones, nothing fancy. I reckon we could open it and reseal it if we're careful.'

'Give it here, I know how to do it, I used to peal open Dad's Giro back in the day. Reckon I've still got the touch.'

Shauna was true to her word, within seconds she expertly opened the envelope and pulled out the white envelope and gave the group a questioning glance.

'We mustn't endanger Brian's life, but I feel if we go in blind then we'll never be free of this. What does everyone else think? We don't have much time.'

'Open the fucker.'

'Agree.' Andy nodded.

The collective gaze then fell on me. Berni was right. This would never be over, but it was a risk. We needed to do it properly and discreetly and now.

'OK. I agree. But we're too exposed here out on the street. Why don't we find a quiet corner somewhere, how about the Central Library? We can open it there, at least there will be people around and a modicum of privacy.'

Red light spells danger

Billy Ocean

Red light spells danger,
Can't hold out much longer
'Cause red light means warning,
Can't hold out I'm burning

6

Chapter

After picking our way across the busy walkways we finally approached the Grade II listed building, the Central Library. Knowing that someone may be following you or have you under surveillance, heightens stress levels and frays tempers. Fortunately, the impressive Library with its showy rotunda and domed structure helped to take our minds off any immediate peril. The design had been loosely derived from the Pantheon in Rome, but there weren't any gladiators here today. Just four very anxious people trying to save a friend. We hurried inside and found a suitably quiet corner.

'Wow, this is fuckin' amazin' for a library. When I was a kid it was just full of druggies and...'

'Not now Shauna, we need to open the envelope. Berni as you're facing the door and have a heightened sense of perception, could you be our lookout? Helena as you're facing the opposite way, the same goes for you. Mouthy, I mean Shauna and I will open the envelope. All ready?' Although Andy phrased these requests as just that, requests - they were rhetorical questions, everyone took on their appointed roles.

2 4

I could see Shauna wriggling with excitement as Andy handed her the envelope. She showed amazing dexterity and within minutes had unsealed it and recklessly shook the contents onto the wooden table. Andy's face blanched with concealed rage as a USB stick skipped across the table towards him Shauna peered inside the envelope and retrieved a piece of blue paper that was folded in half. Hastily Andy retrieved the USB stick and hid it in the inside pocket of his suit jacket, he patted it reassuringly before turning his attention to Shauna.

'Go ahead, we're all listening.'

Shauna gulped, suddenly feeling nervous, heightened by the strong feelings she had for Brian. Andy signalled for her to lower the paper under the table which she did before unfolding it.

'Just one tip Shauna, we don't need your commentary, just read it out.'

'To my dear friends, apologies for leaving you all in such an unfortunate set of circumstances. You are already aware of my demise, in this present world at least. But everything is not as it seems, remember the planning we did during Plenni back in the Watcher 22 days? I will need you to use those collaborative skills once again and work together as a team as that is when we are the strongest.

Our foreign friends must NEVER gain access to this program, it must be protected at all costs. Remember it is not only the future that is at risk it is also our past.

The USB stick is the starting point and each key and message will reveal different clues. This is the only way that I could think of to protect the program and all of you. There is much to do. God's speed and watch your back, my life and death depend upon it.

Regards, Barry.'

'Well, that's as clear as mud. Typical bloody Barry.'

'So is he dead or what?' Shauna asked, still flushed after her spell of public speaking.

'I don't think that this is the time for speculation, our immediate problem is removing the section in the letter that refers to the USB stick. I assume that we all agree that this will not be passed on.' Everyone nodded.

'I agree with Berni, we'll deal with the USB stick back at the house. Let's examine the letter and decide what to do. We don't have much time.'

Shauna carefully placed the letter on the table and pointed to the section that referred to the USB stick. It was, unfortunately, right in the middle of the letter.

'Dammit! We can't remove that part, it would be too fuckin' obvious! Brian's life is in danger....'

'The people who have Brian don't know what this letter looks like or what it will contain right...'

'Jesus! We've been thinking about this all wrong! We don't need to change the letter, we just need to replace it! Is that what you were thinking?'

'Thank you Shauna, it was. This is a library after all, we can either scan in the revised version or write a new letter based on the old one and print it off.'

'Agreed. We need to be as close to the original as possible. They may have other documents of Barry's to compare this with.'

26

'Berni's right. I think we fold the letter carefully to conceal the section about the USB stick, we can then scan it in and print it off. Helena you speak to the librarians and get a scanner and printer organised, Shauna you go with Helena and sort out the scanning. It may take a few attempts to achieve the perfect result. Berni, I think you should remain seated and be our timekeeper and lookout, alert us if you see anything suspicious, and keep us mindful of the time. Helena, you go first and use your teacher's voice if you have to. I'm going to give Brown a call, but don't worry I will head down the high street and bob in and out of the shops. There's no point in sighing Shauna, he was at the will reading for a reason and he does work for Experenta *XP* and he knows more about *Watcher 22* than any of us. Now let's get going.' Andy grinned at me and I nodded in agreement.

I always find library staff to be extraordinarily helpful. I think their characteristics are innate not learned. They always seem to be a very helpful group of people, reasonably direct and always busy, buzzing intelligently around their library hive. These hobbit nurturers will easily deal with our request. I speak to the librarian and after receiving a code and paying a small fee towards printing, we are directed to the IT suite.

I had warned Shauna to remain silent throughout, her choice language would not be tolerated by this very professional team of bookkeepers. Having said that Shauna may be worldly-wise and a tad vocal, but she is also a wizard at IT. She expertly redacted the document, scanned it and printed it out. It was then inserted into the envelope which she gave to me and I zipped it into my handbag. Brilliant. We made our way back to Berni who was now looking quite weary. It was time to leave, we gathered our belongings and headed out towards the glass doors.

That's when it happened. It was so fast. No time to react. A woman came in through the door, her face partially covered with a floral scarf. I glanced at her whilst chatting with the others. Then suddenly, she snatched my bag and ran towards the exit. My purse, my ID and the redacted letter were all gone. It could have been so much worse. But the most frightening thing of all was that the woman knew which bag to snatch. But how? There were three women standing in that doorway, each carrying a handbag and she chose mine. Only someone who was watching and listening could have known that I had the letter. This was a sophisticated operation. Andy was right to speak to Brown, we were out of our depth.

Under pressure

Queen and David Bowie

Pressure pushin' down on me
Pressin' down on you, no man ask for
Under pressure that brings a building down
Splits a family in two, puts people on streets
Mm-ba-ba-beh, mm-ba-ba-beh
Dee-day-da, ee-day-da

7

Chapter

It is always difficult to contain Shauna, but it had to be done. Now was not the time to give chase to the letter thief, we needed to stick together.

'Cheeky bitch! Let me go, Helena! I can get her, the fucker...'

'No Shauna.' Berni said sharply as she turned towards her. There was no mistaking the meaning in Berni's steely gaze.

'We need to stay together. We're already down in numbers, let's just wait for Andy. It's a quarter to four and decisions will soon have to be made.'

'I agree with Berni. Stand down Shauna, there's too much at stake here.'

Before Shauna could disagree, Andy arrived with Brown in tow.

Brown looked annoyed, even when he wasn't. However, today there was no mistaking the red flush of anger that graced his cheeks and the stony glint in his eyes.

'Andy has explained the situation to me. I cannot begin to tell you how dangerous this is. What on earth possessed you...'

Shauna could not contain herself any longer.

29

'Fuck that Brown. Listen up. A woman has just snatched Helena's bag, literally just now!'

'What the hell!' Andy moved towards me.

'I'm fine Andy. Thankfully they only got the redacted version of Barry's letter and not the USB stick, but how on earth did the woman know it was in my bag?'

'Stop talking all of you! We're not safe. Give me your phones, now!' Brown collected every phone and the burner and placed them inside a silver bag. 'We move and we move now!' Brown sprang into action and herded us out of the library and into a nearby Starbucks. He nodded at the barista, who knew him, and we walked to the back of the cafe. Brown tapped a code into the door keypad and held open the door. We all walked in.

'Turn left!' he barked at Berni. 'Through the door on your right. The light switch is behind the door.'

Once we were all safely in the room, the urgency of the situation hit us. Brown put the burner phone on the table only minutes before the clock struck four.

'What if the woman doesn't work for the same bastards that took Brian? We've nothing to give except for the original and...'

'Calm down Shauna. I think you will find that the phone will ring and further instructions will follow. Who answered the phone last time?' Brown said as he took the burner phone out of the silver bag. We all inwardly cringed as we looked across at Shauna.

'Ah well. It must be the same person to answer the phone again. Shauna, put the phone on speaker so that we can all hear.' Brown barked.

The phone rang on cue and we collectively held our breath. The voice was distorted, as before.

30

'I have the envelope. The letter tells me nothing. If I find that this has been tampered with, you will all suffer. Brian stays where he is for now. This will ensure your future cooperation. Make no mistake we are monitoring your movements. Do not underestimate what we are capable of. We know that the next key opens the safety deposit box in two days. We'll keep Brian until then. We will be collecting the second envelope at the exit door of the bank. No chance for any tampering. Keep this phone by you at all times. Arrangements may alter. Brian is alive, for now at least.' The phone clicked off. Minutes later the beeping sound of a text message came through. Shauna looked at Brown who nodded his assent. They'd sent a photograph of Brian, albeit a poor one, holding today's Metro newspaper which gave us some relief. Brown placed the phone back inside the silver bag.

'We need to move again and now!' he said firmly and we left Starbucks at some speed. Two black Mercedes pulled up in front of the cafe and we needed no prompting to climb aboard, Brown was following in the car behind. No one spoke at first. I just kept thinking of Brian and how terrified he must be. Andy was the first to break.

'Where do you think we're going?' he asked quietly.

'Out of the city,' Berni said quietly. 'Somewhere remote I should think.'

'Are we back with MI5? I don't want to go back to fuckin' London, not again, not for a long time, and if we've put Brian in danger or Brown has …'

'We don't know yet Shauna.' Andy interrupted sharply.

It was a relatively short journey. The cars pulled up at what looked like a country house, which was surprising as we were so close to the city. Brown bounced out of the car and opened our car door quickly, signalling for us all to get out. He was now wearing an earpiece. Within minutes we entered the beautiful, brick-built country house. I managed a quick backward glance from the doorway and was able to see the beautiful countryside, albeit for only a few minutes. A perfect hideaway. Brown was wasting no time and we were led past Reception and through an oak door, moving quickly along a well-lit passageway. We then made our way up a circular staircase with polished wooden banisters and then down a corridor lined with plush red carpets and adorned with expensive oil paintings. Finally, we were shown into a lovely suite, tastefully decorated with no expense spared. Brown signalled for us to be seated at a beautiful walnut table and we all silently obeyed.

'From this moment on, we take no risks. Andy did the right thing in calling me.' Brown said whilst flashing a telling look towards Shauna who was uncharacteristically quiet. 'Your friends and family have been informed and whilst they are unaware of your whereabouts, they know you are safe.'

I hear Berni's sigh of relief and an accompanying snort of disdain from Shauna. 'You know the drill. You talk to no one and you must remain here in the suite. Phones are confiscated, obviously and there are no computers and no Wi-Fi, this is all for your protection. There are rooms here for all of you and you may share if you feel more comfortable.' Brown was beginning to calm down a little.

'So it's card games and eye spy again for us Brown. Hope you're bound by the same petty rules as us.'

The short silence was more powerful than any words. Brown turned to give Shauna the full impact of his gaze and she seemed to visibly shrink.

'Well Shauna, it's good to know how thoughtless you can be, especially when you consider the danger that Brian is facing.' Shauna lowered her head and flicked some imaginary fluff off her jumper. Andy sensed that a backlash may be building.

'Brown, can we move on? Please remember that none of us chose to be in this position. Barry named us in his will.'

Brown sighed. 'Well, at least your surroundings and accommodation are four-star you might be a little grateful for that.'

'But our freedom, safety and independence are priceless.' Berni said. We all nodded in agreement.

'This isn't a movie or a reality show, this is real life with danger and real enemies of the state. That is the last I will say on the matter.'

Brown took a deep breath and pushed his chair back from the table.

'Whilst your behaviour has been reckless, we know that for now at least Brian is alive.' At this point Shauna raised her hand, ready to let rip, but Andy shook his head and she relented.

'Andy I believe you have the USB stick? I will need that from you... I can see your hesitation in giving it up. I fully understand the danger that Brian faces, that all of you are facing. I suggest that we await the arrival of MI5's best tech brains as we have no idea what is on the USB stick. It could be a formula that none of us can understand or a code. We cannot risk messing this up, Barry would have known that we would call the experts in to help and may have used a hardware-based encryption system, also sensitive information can be stored in a special password-protected partition on the USB flash drive. This is all the expertise I have and actually, I had this relayed to me. It will be no surprise that I have been in contact with MI5. Their expertise is invaluable. Cagney and Lacey are on their way as we speak.' Brown paused, sensing our disappointment.

Andy raised his eyebrows, but I noticed a flicker of a smile on Shauna's lips. We had spent a lot of time with Cagney and Lacey (not the Agent's real names of course) back in London and we all thought that we had put those days behind us. Life always became so much more complicated and restrictive when MI5 was involved.

'You must understand that Barry's will is not the issue here, it's his ability to travel back through time and potentially alter history. That is the reason for the international interest and the danger that accompanies it. Once the contents of the USB stick have been analysed, I will debrief you. You are all looking a little tired. Dinner will be served here in the suite at 6 o'clock and we will meet up again after that. Two security guards have been posted outside for your safety and also to prevent any night-time wandering.' Again Brown looked over toward Shauna. A dangerous move. Berni reached out and covered Shauna's hand with hers.

'Another time Shauna.' she said softly.

Brown then stood up to leave, 'Bill and Ben are on guard, should you need anything.' and with that, he left the suite and the tension in the room slowly eased.

'We're safe here for now.' Berni said quietly. 'But the danger is real and close by. I think we will have to relocate and soon.'

'Can we have our grub and some bloody sleep first?' Shauna asked crossly.

'I feel that tonight will be fine, for us and for Brian. Tomorrow, however, is quite another matter.'

Berni's insight and instincts had kept us out of danger in the past. Psychic, gifted, or just perceptive, only a fool would ignore Berni's wise words.

One night only

Jennifer Hudson

You've got one night only, one night only
That's all I have to spare
One night only,
Let's not pretend to care

8

Chapter

They say that when you lose one sense, other senses get stronger. Brian was hoping that this was the case. He expected the blindfold, but the plastic ties that secured his hands, cut into his wrists. Brian was pushed across the back seat of the car and told to keep down. Twenty minutes later, after a stint on the motorway, he was dragged out of the car and bundled into a building. His feet crunched on the gravel and there was a faint smell of lavender, which he logged in his memory. They escorted him down a staircase and into a musty-smelling room. He was thrown into a chair, the blindfold removed and a black material bag was placed over his head. His chest was then taped to the chair and plastic cable ties were tightened around his ankles and the chair legs. Then they left. He could hear the sound of a door being locked. No more words had been spoken.

Brian sighed, he allowed himself to let his guard down now that he was alone. He took a few cleansing breaths and then focused on his friend Jerome, a 'nut job' (his words) and survival expert. Jerome had decided to share some tips when they were on a stag do in the Brecon Beacons early last year. Not Brian's idea of fun, but now he has thanking his lucky stars that he hadn't baled. He was relieved to be out of the car but had to use all his power of concentration to stop himself from imagining the different forms of torture that his brain was happy to illustrate in glorious technicolour. Jerome had shown the group how deep breathing can lower your heart rate and reduce blood pressure. He also shared basic survival techniques as they sat around the camp-fire. That was of course before the drinking started. Brian focused on regulating his breathing and positive thinking rather than dwelling on gruesome possibilities. He had no idea where he was. He roughly calculated that he was twenty minutes outside of Manchester, but this was a big City and close to so many motorways and exits. Right now, his location wasn't his biggest problem. Not getting murdered most definitely was. This was a professional crew. He had only heard muffled voices and no clear conversation. He wasn't even sure of the language they were speaking. It felt like a military operation, sadly not one of MI5's. He began to rock the chair, just to test its weight and stability. It wasn't nailed to the floor or on wheels. It was just a bog standard dining chair, without any arms. With his breathing under control, Brian began to consider his escape plan. It was still daylight and he knew that the team would be worried about him. The last thing that he wanted was for Berni, Helena, Andy, or the lovely Shauna to come into harm's way or make rash decisions because he had been captured.

Brian felt certain that he was being held in a regular house, possibly in a cellar underneath a kitchen. He continued with the breathing exercises. The black bag over his head helped with visualisation and he imagined himself back at the camp-fire. He needed to remember Jerome's words of wisdom. It took some time and then Jerome's voice entered his head. It was faint at times, but he remembered most of it and was able to fill in the gaps where necessary.

'In a capture situation act quickly and quietly, whilst you still have the energy and are mentally alert. You may become dehydrated or food deprived and not only does this affect you physically but it also impacts the decision-making process. So act with care and precision, but act sooner rather than later.'

Brian took another deep breath and made a decision, he needed to act quickly.

He listened carefully to check that no one was coming, then he began rocking the chair gently from side to side, picking up momentum, before managing to tip the chair over onto the floor so that he was on his side. There was a cracking noise as the back panel of the chair split into two. Brian's heart was pounding, but he kept going. He managed to roll onto his back and could feel splinters of wood piercing his skin. No matter. There was some give in the tape now and he began lifting his elbows repeatedly to force the tape a little higher. He needed to be able to flex his elbows if he stood any chance of snapping the cable ties. Once there was sufficient manoeuvrability, he visualised Jerome's demonstration. He began by putting his hands together as if in prayer, then making a fist and pulling both fists towards his chest and pushing his elbows out and repeating this very quickly. Jerome had stressed that this method would not work on metal-lined cable ties. Brian had already checked and these were cheap plastic ties.

He could hear noises. They were coming! Brian was struggling, trying to get the force of his body behind him, lying flat on the floor was proving difficult. Maybe he should save the cable tie escape method for another time when he could use it properly. Even if he snapped them, he wouldn't have enough time to hide or surprise them. It would be a waste and then they would know Jerome's method and probably chain him up instead or use handcuffs. Timing was everything. He knew that the captors would have expected him to attempt an escape. Despite his failure to break free, there was one thing that Brian had managed to do apart from impaling himself on wood splinters, he had managed to edge the black bag a little way up his face and now knew for certain that he was in a cellar. No windows, of course, and only one door at the top of the stairs with a halo of light around it.

Suddenly, the room flooded with electric light and noise, as two of the kidnappers ran down the stairs. They still did not speak. The first thing they did was to secure the black bag over Brian's head and neck and tie it securely. The chair was then jerkily up-ended and Brian gasped as some of the splinters of wood snapped, sending shooting pains down his spine. He managed to silence any sounds, not wishing to give the kidnappers any ideas about where they could inflict more pain should they choose to. Brian waited. The silence was unnerving, How were they communicating? He knew that they must be making a plan about what to do with him next, he couldn't be left like this. Then a familiar sound cut through the silence, a mobile phone ringing and very close by. The jingling ring tone faded as one of the kidnappers left the room. Still, no words had been spoken. This might be his chance. There was only one of his assailants in the cellar now. He was desperate to try and engage in some dialogue, not just for his own sanity but also to get some clues. The decision was taken from him. Without warning, pain seared through his back as the tape was stripped off him, ripping out the splinters of wood as it did so. He felt faint, probably a combination of dehydration and pain. Were they going to murder him or move him? He prayed it would be the latter. His head became woozy and a light sweat crossed his brow, he knew the signs only too well. The last thought that crossed his mind before he passed out was an image of Shauna and Helena dancing and laughing as the world was spinning. And very faintly, just in the background, he could have sworn he heard Flint chuckling.

Jailhouse Rock

Elvis Presley

The warden threw a party in the county jail
The prison band was there, and they began to wail
The band was jumpin', and the joint began to swing
You should've heard them knocked out jailbirds sing

9

Chapter

It had been a long night for everyone. Cagney and Lacey were now in situ, accompanied by a significant security team. The global implications surrounding the contents of Barry's will had escalated and now there were new international players involved. The intelligence regarding Brian's' abductors had been inconclusive, but the involvement of foreign powers had not been ruled out. CCTV had also failed to provide any useful results, as had the now disabled tracker, on Barry's phone. The source of the calls on the burner had been expertly rerouted by the captors and as yet could not be traced, the phone messages were still being analysed. This was not some amateur set-up, these were professionals, which meant that the threat level went up another notch and this location was no longer secure.

Needless to say, we were on the move again. This time the operation had all the hallmarks of MI5 involvement. We were woken up in the wee small hours when it was still dark and eerily quiet and we were back on the move. The sun's rays were just beginning to filter through Manchester's new skyscraper skyline in the distance. It was too early for the usual banter, even for

Shauna. Seamlessly we drew up outside the Hilton Hotel close to Deansgate. A huge, stepped column of a hotel boldly grasped for the stars.

'Fuckin mint!' exclaimed Shauna, never one to hide her feelings. 'Now this makes up for all that shite. Have we got a whole floor to ourselves do you think Helena?'

'Shauna, try and control yourself, we're not on holiday. Could we all spare a thought for Brian.' Berni said firmly. I paused and looked down towards my feet, as a mark of respect. Shauna took a moment before the excitement bubbled up inside her again and burst forth.

'It's bloody impressive though Berni, you have to admit it, and right in the centre of town.'

Before any further comments could be made we were whisked from the BMWs, through the elegant lobby and toward the lifts. Cagney was our escort and we all managed to get into one lift. He then produced a silver key which he inserted into the keypad, turned and then pressed the button for floor 25, which was a restricted floor. Shauna still fizzed with excitement and asked repeatedly if we could go to *Cloud 23*, the highest bar in the city.

Cagney turned to face her, clearly annoyed, but she was saved from Cagney's ire by the lift door opening. We were hurried along the corridor and into yet another suite of rooms. The views over the city were breathtaking and even Cagney took a sharp intake of breath.

'Don't get too comfortable here.' Lacey interrupted. 'We had a security breach at the last hotel. It was one of the cleaners we think, so we had to move fast. Brown is on his way to debrief you. There's a lot of planning for the next trip to the bank.' he nodded over to Cagney.

'We'll clear off now, leave you to it, but we'll be next door. There is security outside, so don't try anything stupid.' he addressed the last bit directly to Shauna. As they opened the door to leave, Brown let them pass before entering. Shauna sighed, but just a little too loudly.

'I heard that Shauna.' Brown said before he noticed the glorious view. 'Simply breathtaking.' he turned to admire it fully. It was indeed a wonderful view of a city once associated with such industrial grime and poverty. This metamorphosis, the creation of a new shiny version of itself, would hopefully not be at the expense of the worker bees. The skyscrapers heralded a fresh start, a regeneration, and a gateway to gentrification, but the distant cries from the nightmare slums in Angel Meadow would not be silenced by such glorified gloss and artificial glamour. A city of two halves. At night the homeless awake to beg on the streets, whilst the wealthy footballers and investment bankers are tucked up in their insulated mansions, sipping on smoothies and checking that the electric gates and security cameras are working. Their wealth, a meritocratic reward, serves to keep their dream alive and the outsiders very definitely outside.

Could this new software change the past, make things fairer, stop wars and correct mistakes that cost thousands of lives? We could only hope.

'Helena! If you could stop daydreaming.' Brown's voice cut through her line of thought, like a knife through butter. 'If you could just focus for once and stop staring out of the window. Thank you Berni and Andy for being in the present. As you know your appointment at the bank, to open the second box, is scheduled for 11.30. Barry's captors will want to retrieve the envelope as soon as you exit the building. That simply cannot happen. Not until we know exactly what it contains. We have secured the bank's permission and plan to copy the contents whilst you are both still in the safety deposit room.

'Let's guess who that will be. One of you two nut jobs perchance?' Shauna said, managing to conjure up a half-smile from Lacey. Brown simply raised his hand to silence Shauna, he refused to be drawn.

'We have been fortunate in securing one of our top IT specialists, Kieran. He has access to the fastest and most up-to-date technology. We don't know what Barry has left for us this time and we only have a small window of opportunity to copy it and analyse it before they do. We were going to send doubles in but it's too risky.'

'It means "little dark one".

'What the fuck Berni! What does?'

'It's an Irish name. Kieran.' Berni paused. 'He'll not be safe in there. I have a bad feeling about this Brown.'

'Berni's instincts are normally spot on Brown. She rarely voices them and less so in a group situation like this. You need to listen to her.' Andy said sternly.

Brown looked piqued and then slowly nodded his head. Before he could respond, Andy came back at him.

'And how are you going to get Kieran in and out of the bank if it's being watched by these 'professionals'.'

'We have our ways. I'm not prepared to go into the detail, for many reasons but mainly to protect Kieran. Please just focus on your roles. No slip-ups. Are you clear? The instructions left by Barry may be time sensitive. It may also require the whole team to act and act immediately. Therefore, Shauna and Berni will also need to be at the bank, waiting outside in one of our cars, ready to spring into action if needed. Each person will play a vital role in this exercise. I urge you all to take this very seriously.'

We all nodded, except for Berni. Andy glanced across at her.

'Berni, is there something else that you want to say?' I asked as she was clearly unhappy.

'We don't have time for this.' Brown added impatiently.

'You ignore her at your peril Brown.' Andy said pointedly.

'I've never known Berni's instincts to be wrong.' I added.

'Too fuckin' right.' Shauna agreed, nodding her head.

Brown sighed. 'Alright Berni, go ahead. You have the floor.' Brown waved his hand dismissively and leaned back in his chair. Berni paused and rubbed her forefinger across her lips before speaking.

'There is no logic or evidence to back up what I'm about to say.' she glanced across toward Brown. 'But I would never forgive myself if I didn't speak out. The people who have Brian are ruthless and will stop at nothing to get what they want. If you have decided to conceal someone in that room with the security boxes, then how do you know that they haven't already considered that? I feel that Kieran will be at risk. Conversations may have been intercepted. After all, we had to leave our hotel very quickly due to that leak. These are very clever people who obviously have access to all the latest listening devices and technology.' Berni paused. 'All I ask is that Kieran is given the utmost protection and that you take the threat to his life very seriously. I am unable to give you any solid evidence or scientific explanation for what I have just said, but the feeling is strong and the danger is real.'

Brown looked up. 'Is that it?' Berni nodded.

'Thank you for speaking out. I respect your comments and will advise the security teams to be extra cautious.' Brown paused. 'However, I'm afraid this is a risk we have to take, we need access to that envelope before its contents are stolen or corrupted. It's the best plan we have, MI5 has sanctioned it and Kieran was put in post last night. We need an expert as we have no idea what Barry has left in the second envelope. You two will be nervous enough, without having to respond quickly, access the necessary IT, copy the contents, and then be ready to leave the bank and possibly face the kidnappers again.' he paused. 'Be ready to depart in fifteen minutes.'

And that was that. Berni looked upset, Shauna wriggled uncomfortably, kicking her trainers against the edge of the table, Andy looked strained and my nerves were jangling. And then to crown it all, I heard the strains of a song and a familiar wicked giggle in the background. Flint was still with us and a fan of *Top Gun* at that.

Danger Zone

Kenny Loggins

Highway to the Danger Zone
Gonna take you
Right into the Danger Zone

10

Chapter

Brian regained consciousness very slowly. He had cramp in his thigh and his back throbbed with the pain of his wounds, but it served to remind him that he was still alive. He knew that he was in a car, the boot of a car and that he was being moved. He also remembered the sound of a phone ringing, just before he passed out.

All Brian could do now was to focus on his breathing, he felt claustrophobic, sweaty, and disorientated. The black material bag was not helping, still at least it wasn't a plastic bag, which proved that they needed him alive, for now at least. It seemed like a smooth journey, with none of the stops and starts of city driving. He tried to flex his feet to relieve the cramp, but the space was tight and he was still bound by his hands and feet. Fortunately, they had not replaced the cable ties with the metal ones. He was still in with a chance. The car came to a slow stop. Brian tried not to panic, he had learned all about hyperventilating during his social work training, but never thought he would have to use those methods on himself. Three doors slammed. The boot was wrenched open and two men carried him out. He could tell that they were under the cover of darkness now and judging by the ease at which they carried him, these were strong men, big men. They remained silent. He was taken inside and then downwards, to what he could only assume, was another basement. This time he was dropped onto a mattress on the floor. His foot was shackled to something, probably a pipe of some sort. Again no words were spoken. Brian was relieved, as any clues to the kidnappers' identity may threaten his survival. He held his breath and kept his eyes closed as the material bag was untied and lifted just as far as his mouth, a bottle of water was held to his lips and he drank greedily. Who knew when he would get water again? The bag was then swiftly pulled down and tied around his neck. More footsteps and then he was fairly certain that he was alone again.

After a few deep breaths, Brian felt ready to assess his new surroundings. He listened carefully, but could only hear the faint murmur of voices, definitely male. They had dumped him on his back while they shackled his leg and the pain from the chair splinters was reminding him to move. His instinct was to roll off the mattress towards the exit, but he couldn't as his leg was shackled. This time, however, his chest was not taped to a chair. He managed to roll onto his right side, take the pressure off his back and then move his cable-tied hands to locate the shackle around his foot. He found it and gave it a hearty tug, there was no give in it, none at all. This may not be his moment to snap the cable ties if he couldn't release his foot from the chain.

Perhaps this place was only temporary, they seemed to have left in quite a hurry from the last one. He could imagine Jerome willing him to stay positive. MI5 would be looking for him and he knew his team would never give up. Brian's train of thought was broken by the sound of the door opening and footsteps padding down the stairs. These were softer steps, gentler. Again there was only silence. He was gently pulled into a sitting position and the person sat behind him, but he didn't feel scared. He got a gentle waft of scented soap and the grip on his arm was definitely less intense. This was a woman, he decided. If only he wasn't chained, this could have been his chance to make contact or even escape. The bag was untied and lifted onto the top of his head. Strong hands positioned his head face forward and he obeyed, as he had no wish to see the face of any of his captors. A soft blindfold was placed over his eyes The person moved around assumedly to face him, but fortunately he could see nothing. She then tapped gently on his knee before placing a small plate in his lap. He didn't need telling or tapping twice, he manoeuvred his taped hands and used a pincer movement to grab whatever she had placed on his lap. Success! Food! Some sort of bread roll. He groaned slightly as he lifted it toward his mouth. But survival instincts came to the fore, just as Jerome had said they would. He bolted the food down, swallowing lumps of bread in his panic to sustain himself. He was interrupted by two taps on his arm and was aware that a bottle was being placed to his lips. He would take everything he was offered and gulped down a juice drink, taking as much as he possibly could. Then it was over, the blindfold removed, and the bag pulled back over his head. He prepared for the captor to leave, but his hands were once again guided. This time to the rim of a plastic bucket. Brian knew what that was for and was thankful to retain just a little dignity. Perhaps his stay was going to be for longer than he originally thought.

Jenni took her time returning to the kitchen with the others. She really felt for Brian, he must be so scared. He had been captured to be used as leverage and to make the team hand over the clues to prevent the team from closing down *Watcher 22* for good. Being able to change history, if indeed the program could, may be incredible, mind-blowing, or in the worst scenario catastrophic, cataclysmic depending on who was controlling it. Crytex was the company behind the kidnap and they had recruited agents from different countries. She had been lucky to be selected. There were only five group members based at this particular house, but there were others in different locations who were responsible for surveillance, operations and reconnaissance. At the initial briefing, the importance of concealing their identities and nationalities had been given the highest priority. The training sessions had been compulsory for every team member and it was rigorous. The training at Crytex had components that they had not encountered before, the manual handling training taught them about lifting, lowering, pulling or pushing, anything that could put a strain on the body. They had also been introduced to a range of key signs to use instead of speaking. Interestingly, each member of the twenty-strong team had to experience wearing the material bag over their heads for twenty minutes apiece, whilst the other team members practised communicating with each other using the key signs without speaking. This was much harder than any of them had imagined, but the serious consequences of not employing these tactics could potentially lead to facial recognition and voice biometrics being used in their identification and subsequent capture.

The captors were given very limited information regarding the operation.

There was only one woman in the captors' team of four, and that was Jenni. From the training course, Jenni felt sure that Lars was from a Scandinavian country, judging by his accent. She was also convinced that Maxim was Russian and that Carl was German but with excellent English. Discussion at the training sessions was discouraged and swiftly closed down. Jenni had some medical training and a military background. She took a deep breath before re-entering the kitchen and slipping straight back into the strict silent regime. It was proving to be more demanding than she had originally thought. Lars pointed to a pan of something bubbling on the stove and handed her a bowl. There were bread rolls on the table. Jenni served herself a bowl of hot broth and sat down. She was only two spoonfuls in, when an alarm pierced through the silence and each team member sprang into action. There were no drills on this mission. Something was wrong, the house alarm had been triggered.

Brian heard the alarm too. Could this be his moment? He pushed himself upwards and onto his feet, yanking at the chain that secured his leg. Then came the sound of footsteps, heavy booted footsteps, this was not the woman. He didn't like it, people panic under pressure and mistakes can be made. He was pulled roughly from the bed and pushed up against a wall. A hand covered his mouth making it harder to breathe through the material bag. Brian's heart pounded in his chest, he imagined Berni's face, forced himself to see her, feel her presence, and send her a message asking for help. His future was in the balance and he knew it.

I've Gotta Get a Message to You

Bee Gees

I've just got to get a message to you
Hold on, hold on
One more hour and my life will be through
Hold on, hold on

11

Chapter

There was no time to talk, which was probably a good thing. Even in the new luxurious surroundings, our nerves had got the better of us after Berni's revelation about her concerns surrounding Kieran. Exactly twenty minutes later Andy and I were ushered into the BMW and quickly deposited outside the bank. Shauna and Berni followed behind in another BMW which then overtook us and parked behind the bank. Andy squeezed my hand as we entered and after the usual ID check, Freddie and Andy headed for the security door. I took a seat in the waiting area, making made sure that I had my back to the window and tried to disguise my inner turmoil. This time Andy was much quicker, he was used to the drill.

I was surprised at how soon I heard the heavy slam of the door which signalled Andy's return. There was no disguising the relief on Andy's face. But he did throw me a sideways glance, which I'd seen before. It was definitely a sign, perhaps things had not gone to plan, but it was not the right time to ask. We had to keep up the façade, you never knew who was watching. He reached out for my hand and we headed toward the

5 3

front door. Andy tapped the inside of my palm with his finger, another indicator that something was off. But we had to go through the motions and pretend that everything was normal.

Just as we approached the front door of the bank, I heard the sound of the heavy door slamming and caught a glimpse of a young man, a young man with dark curly hair and he was heading for the fire exit where Berni and Shauna were waiting in the BMW. I looked straight at Andy and mouthed the word, Kieran. He nodded and opened the front door of the bank and motioned for me to go through. It had been Berni's instinct that led us to believe that something may be wrong and she was normally right. We nervously waited for the BMW to collect us. Nothing untoward happened. It drew up to the curb within minutes and still, there was no interception. But something felt off. As soon as we slammed the car door, Andy spoke, 'Brown, radio the other car, the one with Berni and Shauna in! Now! Just do it! I'll explain later. Now drive!!' We sped away, heading in the direction of our friends.

'Dammit! Kieran never got into their car. There was a distraction. A gang of youths blocked the exit and used threatening behaviour. 'Andy, does Kieran have the copy?'

'He does, it was a USB stick he copied and now I'm worried that he may have wiped the USB he gave back to me. Are you sure that this was Kieran, I mean our Kieran, Berni's dark one?'

'He was checked, and vetted by our security team.'

The driver interrupted. 'Alpha 21 are in pursuit. Sounds as though Kieran picked up a ride on a motorbike. Should we follow Brown? Has security been informed?'

'Back up and unmarked cars are in pursuit, Alpha 21 can stand down. Abort and return to the hotel immediately. Andy, give me the USB!' Brown demanded as we screeched around a tight bend. The USB fell between the seats and we both had to disguise a smile as the normally tight-lipped and self-controlled Brown let forth a string of expletives that would make a docker blush. The driver stared straight ahead, obviously not the worst language he'd ever heard.

'Andy put your hand under my seat man! Hurry! I need to check that USB !' Andy undid his seat belt and shuffled to the edge of his seat, clearly uncomfortable as we were travelling at speed. This was not the time to die by being catapulted through the window of a BMW, which probably had bulletproof glass, a gruesome image was beginning to form.

'Helena! Grab my other hand!' Andy ordered as he lowered himself into position and grappled for the USB under Brown's seat. Just as we approached the hotel, Andy found it and Brown snatched it from his hand as we screeched to a halt. Then, uncharacteristically, Brown bolted out of the BMW and into the hotel. Even the driver was taken aback. Andy gave a huge sigh of relief, we had delivered the USB. We just had to hope that Kieran hadn't deleted the data from the original USB. There was little time to compose ourselves before Alpha 21 swooped in and parked behind us. It was time to regroup and check in with Brown.

We arrived at our suite without incident. Cagney and Lacey had both returned from their security duties and looked as anxious as we all felt. Shauna, never one for holding back, went straight in.

'Andy, what the fuck is goin' on?'

'I could ask you the same.' Andy snapped back. 'We followed procedure and Kieran copied the USB as instructed. He was meant to meet you in your car...'

'Ah, you mean that you let the swine out of the building with a copy, you...'

'No need to be so accusatory Shauna. MI5 vet everyone, that's not our remit.'

'Ooh not our bleedin' remit Helena,' Shauna said mocking me. 'Don't start talking like these bastards or you'll end up just like them.'

'It wasn't him. The Kieran that you saw, it wasn't him.' Berni said firmly. She had been very quiet so far.

'How do you know that Berni?' Andy asked gently.

'I just do. You'll see.'

'And the USB stick Berni, do you think it's been wiped?'

'I don't know... my feelings pick up on emotions and people rather than objects and data.'

'50 quid says it's blank. What do you two say.' Shauna said, winking at the two agents.

'That's inappropriate Shauna. We don't gamble on Brian's life.'

'Just trying to lighten the day, you miserable Welsh...' Fortunately the door slammed shut before Shauna could finish her sentence.

Brown sailed in bristling with importance.

'Take a seat around the table, all of you. Cagney and Lacey you can join us.' We all obeyed and I gave Shauna a warning glance.

'The USB stick was not wiped, Kieran or whoever the bastard was, didn't have time. Berni, you were right, your warning signal was spot on and I apologise for not taking more notice of it. From this moment on that will change. There are a series of instructions on the stick and some references that I think only the team will be able to follow, which was good thinking on Barry's part and will also slow the kidnappers down. There's no time to waste.'

Brown then signalled for Lacey to bring over the laptop on the table, loading the USB before swivelling it around for us all to see.

Watching the Detectives

Elvis Costello

She is watching the detectives
"Oh, he's so cute"
She is watching the detectives
Oh, and they shoot, shoot, shoot, shoot
They beat him up until the teardrops start
But he can't be wounded 'cause he's got no heart

12

Chapter

Brian could sense the tension. This house alarm was not one of the common all garden types, it was extremely loud and showed no sign of stopping. The man holding him did not release his grip, not even for a second. It was unnerving to be held up against a wall by a silent captor and especially one he felt to be extremely uptight, his breathing was rapid and his grip fierce. Brian realised that the alarm would bring unwanted attention, not only to the house itself but to the people in it. It was very loud, it reminded him of the twin siren alarm that was accidentally set off at a Women's shelter he once worked at. It had taken them a long while to disarm it, using various codes and a phone call to the local police station to reassure them that all was well. Knowing this made Brian feel worse, as he knew that this type of alarm was designed to alert the public, to quite literally scream out for help.

After what seemed like an age, the alarm stopped and the man holding Brian released his grip, but only marginally. He forced Brian into a sitting position on the mattress but the captor's hand remained firmly clasped over his mouth, Would people come to the door to check on their neighbours whose alarm was so very loud and persistent? He prayed that they would or maybe even alert the authorities. This must be the captors' main fear, that and breaking their silence if they had to interact with the public. Either way, it put them under increasing pressure and maybe mistakes would be made. For now, at least, they would have to think carefully about moving him, especially as now the house had become the centre of attention. Brian listened intently, praying that one of the neighbours would come over, knock on the door and demand entry and discover him imprisoned against his will, in this dark dingy basement. But he was just dreaming. Why didn't they come? Brian began to feel panic rising within him, there may not be any more chances like this. He could hear Jerome's voice in his head, urging him to control his breathing to instil a sense of calm. He had to think logically, how likely was it that someone would come around and check on their neighbours after an alarm went off, especially neighbours that they didn't even know? He tried to put himself in their position. Would he go around to check if it was him?

Before Brian managed to answer his own question, there was the very welcome sound of knocking on the front door which he could hear from the basement. Disturbingly. Brian heard a growl of frustration from his captor, the sound of suppressed anger, and worryingly the first sign of a lack of control. The grip on his mouth tightened. Should he bite him? Push and shove him? Scream out for help? Was this his chance? Adrenalin pumped through his body, his heart was pounding and seemed to bang against his rib cage. The man holding him could sense that Brian was entering the fight or flight stage and tightened his grip around his arm and his mouth. Brian had to do something, no one knew he was down here. An innate desire to survive overtook any logic. He elbowed the captor in the stomach using the force of his tied hands and managed to catch him off guard. Just for a moment, the captor released his grip over Brian's mouth and despite having a dry throat Brian made a noise of sorts. A deep noise emanated from his stomach, indescribable but reasonably loud. The captor recovered and silenced him. Brian took the opportunity to kick his free leg repeatedly on the pipe his leg was chained to and made as much noise as he could. His captor wrenched him onto his back and cracked him hard across the head.

They had sent Jenni to the door. She was reasonably well versed in placating people and resolving conflict situations. The man in front of her was tall, well-built and most noticeably, not smiling.

'In the name of God, is everything alright?' the man asked, his voice edged with irritation. Jenni assured him that all was well, using a calming smile and gentle tones. She'd had the fore-site to tie an apron around her waist and pull up her sleeves, giving the appearance of a busy housewife.

'That's an industrial alarm. This is a residential area, families live here and some pensioners.' he stated directly and in a somewhat accusatory manner. Jenni nodded, exuding understanding and sympathy for his plight. Gradually his tone of voice began to soften. The other captors had been positioned behind the door and they gradually backed away, confident that the situation was now under control.

'I know you've only just moved in and as a member of Neighbourhood Watch, I understand only too well the need for security and safety. These are troubling times and....' Jenni would never know how the sentence would end as the neighbour was interrupted by Brian's great shout, almost a bellow, and the sound of banging which came directly from the basement. Her training provided her with two options. Option Number 1 - make up her 'husband's project' down in the cellar and hope that this guy believed her without going down to see it for himself. Option Number 2 - drag him inside the door, tie him up, and then move location, again. There was Option Number 3, but Jenni didn't want to think about that just now. Before she could decide, the choice was made for her as Carl came up the staircase from the basement. He appeared to be flustered and out of breath, armed with a hammer and looking suitably distracted.

'Everything alright darling? 'Carl asked Jenni, whilst walking towards the kitchen. 'Damn IKEA flat packs. I'm afraid the wardrobe won't be ready tonight or tomorrow by the look of it.' then as an afterthought, Carl turned toward the door. 'Sorry about the alarm. It won't happen again. I've disarmed the bugger. You know how temperamental these things are, it was left by the last owner. It must have been triggered when we turned the power off earlier.'

Neighbourhood Watch man nodded in all the right places, eager to share manly woes and the trials of the flat pack rang true for him.

'I can give you a hand if you like, I'm a dab hand at carpentry...'

Carl casually slung his arm over Jenni's shoulder and she leaned into him as she shook her head.

'Boys and their toys. Honestly, thank you but we are just about to eat.' she said convincingly.

'Well if you change your mind later, I'm next door but one, number 17, just let me know and I can pop round with my tool kit.'

'Cheers mate. But as Jenni said we're about to eat and I'm going to call it a day now. Good of you to call around though. Sorry again about the alarm. Good to know you're nearby and keeping a watch on the area. Take care now.' and with that Carl and Jenni waived him off and gently closed the door. Every rule had been broken and their faces had been seen by a man who would most likely remember them. They had attracted unwanted attention, this went against every directive and could prove to be a mistake that would cost them dear.

Runaway baby

Bruno Mars

Run, run, run away, run away, baby
Before I put my spell on you
You better get, get, get away, get away, darling
'Cause everything you heard is true
Your poor little heart will end up alone
'Cause Lord knows I'm a rolling stone
So you better run, run, run away, run away, baby

13

Chapter

Everyone leaned forward to get the best possible view of the screen.

'Shall I read through it out loud, so we can all follow it together?'

'You can tell she's a bloody teacher.'

'This is not the time Shauna!' Andy snapped at her.

'That would be lovely, thank you, Helena.' Berni said gently. I nodded and began reading.

'If this is the first clue you have, then my plan has worked, I realised that you might not get access to the very first clue, due to the obvious risks involved. The initial clue was bogus anyway. I do understand that I have placed you all in great danger, but at some point, you must have all known that the world would come calling for *Watcher 22* once again. The data shown below is for the Techies, it is the sequence to trigger the shutting down program and has to be entered 10 days before the program can actually be destroyed. Experenta *XP* the parent company, installed this as a kind of fail-safe.' I paused and scrolled down the screen, there were lists of numbers and formulas that meant absolutely nothing to any of us.

'Your next port of call is John Rylands Library. I want you to think back to the early days and my leaving party. Brian was not with us then of course.'

'I had forgotten that.' said Andy. 'It's somewhat fortuitous under the circumstances.'

'You mean coz he's been bloody kidnapped Welshy? Just say it like it is.'

'That's not what I meant mouthy and you know it.'

'Quiet please. Helena, could you continue? Berni asked politely.

'The initials of the title of this famous book can be found by answering these questions.'

'Lacey please write these down.' Brown ordered and Lacey responded.

'My first is the initial of the first name of the team member who played Tom Jones at the Plenni party?' Lacey paused.

'It was me!' Andy shouted enthusiastically.'

'So the first initial of the book title is A. The second initial is the first initial of Shauna's character.' again I paused.

'Ooh ooh. Let me answer!' Shauna said excitedly. 'It was me! I was Aubrey, Aubrey Heartburn or summat.'

'Thank you, Shauna. You played a stunning Audrey Hepburn.' I looked around ensuring no one laughed. They didn't.

'So now we have AA. Please carry on Lacey.'

'The third initial is the second letter of the actress's first name.'

'It's U!!' Shauna shrieked so loudly that Lacey nearly fell off his chair.

'Once you have established the title of the book, it's time for the final clue.' 'We are looking for a book title with three words that begin with AAU.' Berni said calmly.

'Fuckin' brilliant! What use is that to us?'

'You need to remember Shauna that only we know those answers to the questions Barry asked. That's clever. The kidnappers will be stumped right now. Any further clues Helena?'

'Yes. The next clue is Berni's middle name.'

'But I never use it. It's not on any of my documents.'

'That's good Berni. But if it's on your birth certificate we need to move fast.'

'Well, I don't know how Barry would have known…'

'Stuff that Berni. Just tell us!'

'Yes, yes course.' Berni paused. 'It's Alice.'

'Bingo. Alice.' Andy paused. 'Hey, I wonder if it's Alice in Wonderland?'

'But it's AAU smarty pants, not AIW.'

'Whose phone is quickest? Shauna, it's probably yours. Do a search for Alice in Wonderland at John Rylands library.'

'It's not coming up! Shit. It must be called something else.'

'I think that Lewis Carol started with a different title. I can't quite remember…'

'That's great Berni. Shauna type this into the search - what was Alice in Wonderland originally called.'

'Yes boss. Am on it. My spelling is a bit dodge, but I'm on it. Here we have it. Alice's Adventures Underground!! AAU!'

'Nailed it! Brilliant work!! Well done Andy. That will take the kidnappers time to sort out, especially if they come from other countries.'

'Well done Shauna. You did really well …'

Lacey interrupted. 'There is something else. I don't think that just finding the book will give us the message. Listen to the last instruction.' Lacey waited for madam to settle down.

'Finally, find the author's date of birth, add the numbers together and then add the number of Alice books that were published and this will give you the page number. Once you find the book, copy that page and use the code below to retrieve my message. And yes Shauna I could have copied the page of the book in question and inserted it below. The reason for all the subterfuge is to throw off the bad guys and make sure that only the team can access the codes to destroy *Watcher 22* and ensure that the world and its history remain unchanged.'

Shauna was for once, taken aback. 'He mentioned my name.' she looked shocked.

'He's dead Shauna, not a God! And also it wasn't that complimentary...'

'Right let's move..' Brown said sensing the tension in the room beginning to rise. Andy used his phone to locate Lewis Caroll's date of birth.

'1832. Lewis Caroll was born in 1832. Add that together and it's 14 and we know there were only 2 Alice books published so it's 16, page 16!'

'Excellent work. I think that the group should stay together. But Berni and Shauna should enter the library with Lacey. This book is a famous one and to gain instant access we may need to use the MI5 card. Helena and Andy have been seen by the kidnappers, they will remain in the car in case they are needed. Cagney will organise the transport.' Brown nodded over to him and he left at some speed. Lacey will escort you into the building and remain as protection. Let's go!'

'We could chuffin' well walk there from here. It's only about ten minutes and God knows we could use some fresh air. How about it Brown?'

'Do I need to remind you that we have already lost one member of the team on the so-called 'friendly' streets of Manchester? I have no intention of losing another. Not on my watch!'

'Crikey keep your hair on, for f…'

'Not now Helena. Let's just go and get the book as Barry has requested.' Berni said quietly.

'Is everything alright Berni?' I asked gently.

'To be honest Helena. I don't know. I have a bad feeling about Brian, it's only a feeling but…'

'What about Brian, Berni? Tell us. We know about your feelings!'

'I think…. I think he may be in pain.'

'Right, that's quite enough! Even more reason to move quickly. I won't ask again. Lives are at stake here.'

'Why aren't your lot looking for him? Surely they must have found somethin' by now?' Andy asked, clearly upset.

'I'm not at liberty to say and even if I was…'

'You don't fuckin' know!'

'Shauna this isn't the time. Let's go and at least follow the only thing we have, the clues that Barry left for us.'

Somebody's Watching Me

Rockwell

I always feel like somebody's watchin' me
And I have no privacy
I always feel like somebody's watchin' me
Is it just a dream?

14

Chapter

Brian had only been knocked out once before in his life and that was when he was thirteen. High school had been a shock to the system after the cosiness of primary school. Inevitably the 'bigger boys' fought hard to protect their playground territory and that's exactly where he came up against Jonny Leadbetter or Jonny Deadbeat as he was known. Only the bravest of the brave called him that though and Brian was not in that category. He had spent his time keeping his head down and avoiding confrontation. Brian's reputation as a peacemaker had long since faded, along with so many other childhood dreams. But one Friday, close to the end of term, he had been in the wrong place at the wrong time. Everyone knew the dangers of crossing the quad, it was Deadbeat territory, but Brian had been swept away with end-of-term fever. A long ball from his friend sent him careering into dead man's land. An ominous hush spread through the throngs as Brian backed unknowingly into Jonny Leadbetter. Brian knew that if he was to stand any chance at all, he had to show no fear. Jonny yanked him around, sneering at him and kicking the ball away into the low-lying shrubs. Eye contact was not recommended, but Brian had no time to compose himself. He faced up to the bully, feigning confidence and praying for a reprieve. That was a mistake and Jonny was not the forgiving kind. He took Brian's defiance as a call to arms and threw him a punch that sent him to the ground. The side of Brian's head took the impact and smacked against the tarmac. The world went black.

Memories of the school-yard flooded back to him and he could almost taste the blood in his mouth. He shook himself back to the present, willing himself to wake up, but there was no light and no familiar sounds. His head throbbed and he was struggling to come around. He opened his eyes, but darkness prevailed. The smothering feel of the material bag and the realisation that his hands and feet were still tied, firmly established his captive status. He had no idea if he had been moved again, but knew that he would be treated less sympathetically after making a scene. Brian was right. The next person to visit was very different and very definitely not a woman. If a punch in the head was the only price he had to pay for his antics, then he felt he had got away lightly. For now, they still needed him, once all the clues had been located, things would be very different. There was no point in thinking about it now. As far as he could tell they were still only on the second clue, so time was on his side. Gone was the gentle touch and care that the woman had employed, this visitor was a man, he was sure of it. The lively smell of Lynx Africa and the heavy-handed removal of the material bag left him in no doubt. There was a sense of unspoken anger, he could feel it. From now on he needed to be a model prisoner, the escape plan would have to stay on hold until the perfect opportunity presented itself.

Brian was fed and watered with heavy, clumsy hands. He felt as sure as he could that he hadn't yet been moved. He didn't have a lot to go on, but the bed felt the same, but he was now chained to something different, not the pipe, something higher up on the wall. He would investigate once the new jailer had departed. The unpleasantness with the bucket was then completed, the details of which Brian did not dwell on. He eagerly awaited the hefty man's departure, but it didn't come. Instead, something much more unpleasant came his way. The material bag was lifted again and then he felt the sharp pain, as a needle was driven deep into his neck. There was that familiar heady smell of felt pens and next came the woozy feeling, made worse by the complete darkness inside the material hood. Brian knew he was about to lose consciousness, this was his punishment for his noisy behaviour, for trying to get attention, to get help. Where were they, his friends, the team, MI5, when would they come? This was the last question he asked himself before disappearing into the velvety blackness.

The 'angry' man was Maxim and he was very angry, just as Brian had suspected. He checked that Brian was completely out before returning upstairs. The meeting began in hushed tones, in keeping with the strict protocol which had been drilled into them during their training.

'He's out cold. Probably for the next eight hours. Before then we decide how to proceed. My instinct is to cut and run, but our next safe house isn't ready, we have only just arrived, so...'

'So we stay here for now. 'Jenni interrupted. 'You did a great job Carl, with Neighbourhood Watch Guy.

But he's a bit of a busy body, do you think he'll come back with his tool kit?'

'I do.' Carl said, nodding his head.

'As I see it we have three choices.' Maxim said, 'Number one - we simply remove that busybody from the equation.' he mimed the action of slitting his throat and Lars smiled and hopped from one leg to the other with glee.

'Number two - we move to that safe house, but maybe greater risk. Or Number three - we act our way out of it. I know what I prefer.'

Lars could barely control his excitement. Jenni felt sick. This was not what she had signed up for. Carl was the next to speak,

'I agree that our choices are limited and that we must be very careful. If the Neighbourhood Watch man is killed and we disappear, that will surely arouse suspicion with the authorities. I think a better plan would be to find out a bit more about him, if he's married, does he live alone. Then we make the decision.'

'I agree to this delay on one condition, we decide today. I will take Lars and we will check out the Neighbourhood Watch man. We go now.'

Maxim was never one for pussyfooting around, within seconds they'd grabbed their coats and were gone. Jenni looked across at Carl, there was a definite cloud crossing his sunny features, he and Jenni were alike. Taking care of Brian was the main role and someday soon Jenni hoped Carl would be on her side. Carl shrugged his shoulders.

'Let's just see what they come back with, then we decide.'

They didn't have to wait very long, Neighbourhood Watch guy only lived next door but one.

'There were children's bikes on the lawn, a family Range Rover on the drive and the washing line had kids' clothes on it. He is a family man, so it's more risky taking him out.' Maxim said disappointedly. Everyone nodded in agreement and Jenni sighed in relief.

'I think he may have noticed us walking passed his house, but it's Jenni and Carl that he can identify. I believe him to be he is a nosey man. He will come back, and soon.' Maxim said as he kicked the side of the table in anger.'Come! We prepare. We buy flat pack bookcase and if he comes before this just get rid of him.'

'Maxim's right. If he comes today, we won't answer the door. Tomorrow we half finish the bookcase and leave it in the lounge ready for his visit, let's go.'

'He is lucky he has children. Otherwise ...' Maxim drew his finger across his neck again, much to Lars' delight. This plan had to work.

Sweet Child O' Mine

Guns N' Roses

She's got a smile that it seems to me
Reminds me of childhood memories
Where everything was as fresh as the bright blue sky
Now and then when I see her face
She takes me away to that special place
And if I stare too long, I'd probably break down and cry
Whoa, oh, oh
Sweet child o' mine

15

Chapter

There was a feeling of excitement in the car as they made the short journey to John Rylands Library. Andy read the team a little about the history and they were genuinely amazed to learn that John Rylands himself was Manchester's first multi-millionaire, owning the largest textile manufacturing concern in the United Kingdom.

'At least he didn't depend on the bloody FA and the 'beautiful game' for his livelihood.' Shauna said cynically.

'Ah well, don't forget about the working class, you know the weavers on the shop floor would have had a hard life. I wonder what tales they could tell?' Andy said thoughtfully.

'It did say in the research that Rylands not only gave money to charities discreetly, he also maintained orphanages and provided a town hall, public baths, a library, and a coffee-house in the town of Stretford, where he lived.'

'Fair play to the dude. Especially in the olden times, before Marcus Rashford...'

'Shauna, really, I'm not sure we should be using Rashford as a historical marker.'

'Anyhow, it was his wife that had the library built for him, after he popped it. Not a bad memorial is it?' Andy said as the cars slowed down and glided to an effortless stop outside the front of the library. They all got out and were amazed by the beautiful building. 'It's stunning, simply stunning!' Berni exclaimed. Even Shauna looked overwhelmed.

'Jesus it's breathtaking. It looks like a church.'

'A church crossed with Hogwarts!' A typical Shauna comparison.

'Last bit of info.' Andy said enthusiastically. 'You were right to say it looks like a church Berni, it was designed to resemble a church. It's a Grade I listed building with its neo-Gothic style. Look how it dominates the area with its pointed arches and small windows.'

'It's fuckin' amazing and so is Wikipedia Andy.' Shauna said smiling to herself.

'It is wonderful.' Berni said quietly.

Lacey guided Shauna and Berni passed the front of the library. They turned right passing one of the towers and admired the dark red Barbary stone which had been used to withstand the chemicals in the atmosphere of this once 'filthy town'. There had been many critics who complained that the pollution from the burning of coal and gas made Manchester an undesirable location for valuable manuscripts. But with typical Northern ingenuity, by 1900 the ventilation system had evolved to include electric fans to draw in air at pavement level and spray it with water.

The team walked down by the side of the library and towards the modern extension. Berni, Shauna and Lacey then entered the library and approached the reception desk. Lacey took charge, arrangements had already been made which meant that the usual three-day notice period and strict rules for viewing historical books had been waived, such was the power of MI5. They were cleared to enter and boarded the lift which took them to the fourth floor. On arrival, Lacey showed his ID and they were buzzed in. Coats and bags were usually kept in lockers, but the normal protocol had been bypassed and the Special Collections reading room had been cleared of any other visitors. Even Shauna appeared to be bubbling with excitement as Julie, one of the Special Collections team, buzzed them into the reading room and brought out the treasured book, 'Alice's Adventures under Ground' which was placed in pride of place on a large cushion. It took Berni a while to get Shauna under control when Julie introduced the 'snakes'. Book snakes are metal beads encased in a soft cotton sleeve and are designed to help hold books open on certain pages, to avoid direct contact, and also to free up the researcher's hands. Julie demonstrated how to use the snakes and then returned to the office.

'Come on Berni, tame your snake, and let's get this page copied.' Shauna always had a way of spoiling the magic. Lacey carefully located pages 16 and 17 in the 'Alice's Adventures under Ground', (Artist's Choice Editions 2013) and was able to take photographs as this had also been cleared by the Collections team.

'These beautiful sketches are all by Lewis Carroll and have been hand coloured by Ian Beck.' Berni said in amazement, as she carefully turned the pages.

'It's a real pleasure to see this and…'

'Enough, we need to leave.' Lacey said abruptly. For a moment the team had enjoyed a little respite, but now it was back to business. They packed up, thanked the team, and on request Lacey allowed the team to make their way down the beautifully carved, stone staircase, the arches were decorated with delicate quatrefoils.

It felt like they had entered a different world, one they were in no hurry to leave.

'Lacey, could we please cut through the Historic Reading Room on our way out?' Berni asked gently

'OK, follow me, talk to no one, keep your pace in line with mine, and don't draw any necessary attention to us. Lacey ordered whilst flashing Shauna a warning glance. It was difficult to remain on task as they walked through the iconic Reading Room. It had the feel and the layout of a church, with its beautiful stained glass windows and rich red carpet. The reading alcoves were designed for private study but are always open to anyone. A truly outstanding and beautiful library built in the centre of an industrial city. Even Shauna was taken aback.

'So anyone can come here! Even commoners like us?'

'Stop dawdling! Remember why we're here! Move it you two! We've got a code to break and a friend to rescue!'

Lacey hurried them along the arched corridor into the bright glare of reality.

The cars were waiting and took them back to the hotel with their precious cargo. Lacey wasted no time in assembling the group and loading the pictures onto the computer, projecting them onto a screen with Barry's code alongside. Now was the time to work out what the message was before the kidnappers got to it first.'

Lacey imposed the grid that Barry had provided over the text and within the first two lines the name of the location became clear. Lindisfarne Priory. He then asked the group to scan through Page 17 and Berni spotted the word Northumbria. This sealed the deal.

'Who's Linda and where's her soddin' farm and why did Barry want us to know about it?' Shauna asked impatiently. Berni quietly explained.

'Lindisfarne is a place Shauna, with a famous priory, which is a kind of monastery. As far as I can remember Lindisfarne is a mysterious tidal island off Northumberland's coast and when the tide washes over its causeway it becomes inaccessible.'

'Jesus so we could get stuck there with a load of monks!' Shauna overreacted as usual.

'I don't think we need to go there right now Shauna. Barry is starting to reveal his plan and that's the location. We will need a lot more information and instruction from the clues before we can act.'

'Helena's right. It looks like Barry is preparing us for some sort of final showdown.'

'All this to potentially destroy *Watcher 22* or at least find out more about its capabilities.' Berni said thoughtfully.

'We need to get the next clue tomorrow and see where that leads us.' Lacey said calmly.

'Are we any closer to finding out where Brian is and rescuing him?' Berni asked anxiously. Brown spoke for the first time since he had entered the room, 'There are things we are not at liberty to disclose. But I can now reveal that one of our agents is in close contact with the kidnappers and Brian is still with us, for now at least.'

No one

Alicia Keys

I don't worry 'cause
Everything's going to be alright
People keep talking they can say what they like
But all I know is everything's going to be alright

16

Chapter

Two days after Brian's outburst, the Neighbourhood Watch man visited us. Brian was now sedated during the day. He was allowed to eat, stand up and relieve himself for one hour every evening. Brian was closely supervised by Maxim, the sternest and hardest member of the group. With Brian now posing no threat, attention had been paid to the IKEA bookcase, screws had been deliberately lost and the shelves were rammed into position, clearly at the wrong angle. Appropriate tools were laid strategically on the carpet. It was a poor job, but looked convincing and would no doubt cause the Neighbourhood Watch man to spring into 'repair mode' and complete the job.

On his arrival, Lars and Maxim scrambled upstairs to hide out of view. Carl and Jenni took a deep breath and braced themselves before opening the front door and letting him in. He had his trusty tool kit in hand as expected. They made their introductions using previously agreed false names.

'Lead me to it.' The Neighbourhood Watch man, 'Steve', said enthusiastically as he entered the house. He began heading toward the stairs that led down to the cellar, before being swiftly redirected toward the lounge. Had he noticed the padlock on the outside of the cellar door? That was a rookie error on Maxim's part as Steve was no fool. There was no time to dwell on it.

'Ah, so you decided to work on it on site up here, to save carrying it up the stairs from the cellar once it's completed. Good move. Now then, what have we here?' Steve approached the bookcase with an air of expertise, shaking his head in despair.

'All is not lost, my friends but we do need to start over.'

Jenni went into the kitchen to put the kettle on, while Carl and Steve worked on the bookshelf. On her return, she noticed Steve was looking very smug. He swiftly removed the misplaced screws and banged away happily to release the shelves that had been deliberately sabotaged.

'It's a good job that I came when I did,' he said confidently. 'and with my tool kit. You seem to have some screws missing but I always have spares.' Steve rummaged around and located the correct screws and within what seemed like minutes, he had the bookshelf upright and shipshape. 'All done and now to have a well-deserved cuppa. Thank you. Shall we sit?' he indicated towards the sofa and Jenni dutifully perched on the arm, sipping her tea. Carl sat opposite on one of the armchairs, trying to look relaxed as he made light conversation. Carl stroked back his slick black hair and feigned friendliness in this very awkward domestic role-play. All was going swimmingly until Steve began to field more direct questions. He was quite persistent, but Carl had the measure of him and manage to deflect most of the questions easily. Carl seamlessly switched the focus away from himself and onto Steve.

'You are good with your hands Steve. I don't think that you developed those skills as part of the Neighbourhood Watch programme. What are you doing for your day job?' This was a good question and any information may prove useful, Jenni thought as she maintained eye contact and a demure smile.

'Presently I work as a security guard at Manchester Airport, it's only a thirty-minute commute and although the hours are a tad antisocial, it fits in with me and the missus. She's a Nurse, so we manage to work our shifts around the kids.'

Jenni jumped at the chance to keep Steve's focus on his family, rather than probing into their background.

'How many kids do you have Steve?'

'Just the three, I think we'll stop now the youngest is at school. But they keep us on our toes and that's why we decided to stay in one place, for the kids.' Carl began to shuffle around in his seat a little. Alarm bells were beginning to ring.

'How's that Steve? Were you being relocated around the country with your last job?'

'You could say that.' Steve paused for dramatic effect, it worked, as he had no idea just how much depended on his answer.

'You must tell us Steve!' Jenni said somewhat impatiently.

'OK then. We were both in the RAF and we met on the base. One thing led to another, we married, lived in married quarters and we were perfectly happy. But once we began planning a family, Janine stood her ground. She didn't want to be left on the base alone with a baby, not for months at a time. So we both gave notice and here we are. I miss it of course, but the family comes first.'

Carl flashed Jenni a look. She knew what he was thinking. Steve was a danger to them all, he had military training. Not only would he have retained a certain amount of physical resilience, but he would also have been trained to be perceptive and mentally alert. This was unfortunate and to compound the problem, his wife also had military experience. The children had given Steve a short reprieve, but this was a double blow and Maxim was brutal. Jenni had never liked Maxim and now feared, that on hearing this news, he would react without any more delay.

Carl knew what Jenni was thinking, he also hated bloodshed and knew they would have to act quickly to save Steve and his family from harm. Knowing this, they played for time and kept Steve talking. It worked for a while, but Steve was a busy man and soon sprung back into action and grabbed his toolbox. But as luck would have it, Steve unknowingly saved himself and his family right at the very end of his visit.

'I know you're new around here.' Steve said in a measured tone. 'But as you're such close neighbours, could I ask you just to keep an eye on our house?

We're taking the kids to Centre Parcs for a three-day break. We leave tomorrow, early start. If you could just watch the place, it would make me feel better.'

Jenni could have kissed him. Carl assured him that they would be vigilant and would do a regular security check until the family returned from their holiday.

It was all going so well. Right up until they reached the front door. And then it happened. Steve reached out to shake Carl's hand. Carl was left-handed and normally had situations like this well under control, he had long since learned to shake hands with his right. But this was no normal situation and just for a second he reached across with his left hand, his sleeve slid back as he reached across and although he quickly switched hands, there was a split second when Carl thought Steve had seen it. He knew he shouldn't have been wearing it, but it was so reliable and also his lucky mascot, up until this moment. Carl had been so excited when he had finally earned the right to wear the UX diver's watch, after a spell working with the German special police unit. Carl looked over towards Jenni, she had seen it that was obvious. But had Steve seen it and if so would he recognise it to be a renowned military watch and if he had what would his next step be? One thing was crystal clear, Maxim must never find out.

If I could turn back time

Cher

If I could turn back time, if I could find a way
I'd take back those words that've hurt you, you'd stay
If I could reach the stars, I'd give 'em all to you
Then you'd love me, love me, like you used to do
If I could turn back time

17

Chapter

As soon as Steve left the house and the door was closed, Carl took Jenni to one side.

'You can't tell Maxim, not about the watch. You just can't Jenni. My life may depend on it. Steve might not have seen it and even if he did, he might not have recognised it.'

'He did see it and I think a nosey parker and RAF military type like Steve, would either recognise the watch or be curious enough to Google it.'

Jenni peered out of the window and watched Steve turn down the road and walk towards his own house.

'But what would that even mean, what can he use that information for?'

'The risk is this Carl, if Steve gets suspicious and begins to watch us he may gain enough information to alert the police. And let's be honest he probably has police contacts due to his Neighbourhood Watch status.'

'But he has nothing to go on and no evidence that anything dodgy is going on. It's all based on his word and his instinct which is, in this particular case, spot on. I say we keep quiet about the watch, and just focus on Steve's imminent departure. Anyway, the police will have seen loads of busybodies like Steve over the years and...'

They were interrupted as Maxim and Lars bounded down the stairs. Carl shot Jenni a warning glance before the inevitable interrogation began.

Maxim was thorough and direct in his questioning, Lars less so. Carl focused on Steve's trip to Centre Parcs and their new-found role as Neighbourhood Watch delegates. But Maxim was no fool.

'Do you think Steve suspects anything, anything at all that would make him report us? We cannot afford mistakes. I can easily eliminate all five of them tonight, no problem.' Maxim waived his hand as if he could wipe out their lives as if by magic.

Jenni stepped in. 'Steve's leaving Maxim, for three days and by then the safe house should be ready. That's all we need to concern ourselves with. We'll watch his house and then we will be on our way soon after.'

'Jenni's right Maxim. If you did destroy this family, not only would that be unnecessary and cruel, it would also attract unwanted police attention and we have no safe house to run to.'

Maxim seemed unconvinced, but then Lars finally spoke.

'Let Steve take his family away and push for the safe house. A family massacre would be a disaster right now, even though it would be very easy.' Lars couldn't resist a twisted smile as he imagined the scene. Carl and Jenni agreed, trying not to be too enthusiastic which would alert Maxim's highly trained bullshit radar.

'I want you all to note my doubts about this decision. For now, I always keep my pistol and silencer hidden, in case I need them. If I feel we are receiving unwelcome attention or if Steve unexpectedly returns or runs to the authorities, I won't hesitate. Do I make myself clear to you?'

Everyone nodded. It was perfectly clear. Jenni didn't dare look at Carl, in case Maxim sensed something was up or gleaned something through osmosis. He was a perceptive, menacing, and aggressive agent, who should be feared.

There were many reasons for Jenni's deep concern, not just because she harboured great responsibility for the mission, but also for the safety of the world as we know it. It's time to reveal that Jenni is a 'sleeper agent' working for MI5. Knowledge of her true identity would almost certainly result in Maxim cutting her throat or shooting her with his silent pistol. She had been living and working undercover for a long time, desperate to infiltrate *Crytex* and be offered a mission with them, and now at last she had been called to arms. Although Jenni felt that she had the measure of Carl and Lars, Maxim was an unknown quantity and his unpredictability made him a constant threat. Jenni had met Carl on the induction programme. She was familiar with Lars, but this was her first time working with Maxim. He had a military background and absolutely no scruples, which made him a great assassin but a poor agent. She knew that the situation had become unpredictable and the time had come to make contact with MI5. In the wee small hours, Jenni activated the contact by sticking a flyer, advertising the services of a part-time gardener, on the lamp post opposite the house. This was a pre-arranged signal. The street and more importantly the lamp post was monitored by CCTV. The sticker prompted an emergency meeting at a designated time and location, all of which had been preplanned. All Jenni had to do tomorrow was to get out of the house unnoticed, not be followed, and avoid being shot by Maxim.

Meanwhile, safely back at home, Steve was oblivious to the discussions regarding his continued existence. Anyone who has ever tried to pack and organise a family trip will understand exactly how time-consuming the task is. Overexcited children, packing the colour coordinated cases and leaving the house in a reasonable condition and of course rechecking the car and travel sweets, water flasks, and flash-lights..... you get the picture. Steve had not been an aircraft mechanic in the RAF without retaining some of his organisational skills. Janine was equally talented on the planning front and together they proved a formidable team. Even their children had picked up good habits and were reasonably well disciplined, despite the usual sibling rivalry. So amidst this veritable whirl of excitement and an evening departure, the question remains, did Steve see the watch and make the connection with the military and if so was he going to inform the authorities?

Steve had a very ordered mind and categorised things accordingly. There was nothing wrong with his memory. He had learned to record things in precise detail which helped to avert one of his worst fears, making a mistake. And yes, of course, he had seen the watch, he wasn't an idiot. Steve's initial response was that it was an exclusive piece and an expensive one, which did seem a little out of character considering the couple's apparent means. All Steve knew was that it bothered him. In the past, he would have had to research the watch there and then or it would have gnawed away at him until he was satisfied with the answer. Then he became a husband and father and his priorities changed. He learned to pick his battles and to file things away that were annoying or that just didn't sit right, to be retrieved and returned to a later date. This meant that his priorities had changed, the details about the watch were logged for now, but they were definitely not forgotten. He would re-evaluate this strange scenario, and remember the look of fear in Carl's eyes when he pulled down his sleeve and he would do it sooner rather than later.

Good Things Come To Those Who Wait

Nathan Sykes

That's why I take my time
Take as long as I got
Won't pretend to be somebody I'm not, no
Good things come to those who wait
I'm not perfect, nobody is
Could fill an ocean of blood sweat and tears, yeah
Good things come to those who wait

18
Chapter

The very next day Andy and I were ushered into the BMW and quickly deposited outside the bank. It was time to collect Clue 2. Time was of the essence. Shauna and Berni remained back at the hotel. We followed the usual procedure and after the usual ID check, Freddie and Andy headed for the security door, whilst I took a seat in the waiting area.

Andy was even quicker than last time. We were all aware of how time sensitive it could be and with Brian now kidnapped it had upped the stakes. Andy smiled confidently at me before whispering,

'Don't worry Helena this time there's no clue to steal. I just read the clue and remembered it. I will need to write down the instructions once we get to the car.' We were soon back in the car and fortunately, we had not been intercepted. We were probably being watched, but maybe for now the kidnappers had other things on their minds. Brown provided pen and paper, Andy wrote some notes as we headed back to the hotel to meet the others. Once the group was assembled, Andy read the instructions.

'Listen up. Our next destination is The Bridgewater Hall and we have to get a programme and a special envelope from Simon on the main desk. I think the clue will be in the envelope. What I don't understand is why the kidnappers didn't stop us at the bank this time.'

'I think I may be able to answer that.' Brown said as he stood up and took the floor. 'The kidnappers know that security has been increased both in and around the bank. CCTV means that they risk blowing their cover. We believe that they have changed tactics and are tracking the BMWs. We will use different cars from this moment on. It is likely that they are now aware of our location.'

'For fuck's sake Brown! Let's get out of here, we're sittin' ducks.'

'Calm yourself, Shauna. We believe that at present they are distracted by other issues and are now focusing on surveillance rather than abduction or close contact. This is going to be the weak link in the chain for us. Once you have retrieved a clue, we will need a bulletproof exit strategy.'

'Do you have to use the word bullet, Brown? It does ramp up the fear factor.' I said, whilst keeping a close watch on Shauna who had started kicking the side of the table, her Converse trainers tapping a rhythm that indicated a rise in anxiety levels.

'Are we all going?' Shauna asked impatiently. 'I've been stuck in here for ages. It's a lovely room and all, but I'm going stir-crazy. Bloody Barry with his fucked up sense of...'

'Thank you for your input, Shauna. 'Brown interrupted her tersely. 'The decision has been made to send you...'

'Just me! I mean I want to get out of this soddin' room but...'

'Just let me finish Shauna.' Brown paused, but not before shooting her a look of annoyance. This was never a wise move. I placed my hand on Shauna's shoulder to calm her. She shrugged it off and I looked across at Berni who had already picked up on the rise in tempo.

'Shauna will be accompanied by Cagney and Berni. Andy and Helena are known to the kidnappers from their visits to the bank. If we have any chance of a swift and safe mission then we need to reduce the risks by reducing the triggers and targets that are already known to the kidnappers. It's not perfect but we have no choice and need to act quickly.' Brown paused for effect. 'We go later today. Cagney will brief you and I'll see you on your return.' Brown put his paperwork in his briefcase and left the room.

'What the hell are we letting ourselves in for? Will you be packing Cagney?' Cagney looked down at his shoes. Berni just looked confused.

'She means will he be armed Berni.' I explained quietly. Lacey answered quickly.

'Shauna, just concern yourself with your job. You will be protected. For now, that's all you need to know.'

'So that means yes.' Shauna said under her breath.

'What time should we be ready Cagney?' Berni asked a little nervously.

'We leave at 4.30 as the booking office closes at 5 o'clock and we don't want to arouse any undue suspicion. Simon has been briefed, but it all has to look like business as usual.'

'That's in an hour!' Shauna said excitedly.

'We're not going there to watch a show Shauna. Calm yourself and listen closely to the instructions.' Andy said sternly. He was trying to keep Shauna on an even keel. It was always better to distract Shauna when her nerves began to jangle, Andy and I had done a little research and decided that it was a good time to share.

Andy started by showing Berni and Shauna a range of photographs of The Bridgewater Hall.

'It cost around £42 million to build and hosts over 250 performances a year. And impressively the hall is home to The Hallé Orchestra and the Hallé Youth Orchestra. But best of all Shauna, this bit is just for you, get this! It says that the main auditorium sits on a foundation of earthquake-proof isolation bearings that insulate it from noise and vibration from the Metro and road traffic noise!'

'Andy, are you trying to freak us out? Is there a chance of earthquakes as well as being shot at?'

'Of course not you dafty.' Andy said while stroking her arm. 'I just thought that some facts and statistics would make the trip a bit more interesting.'

'Might be for you Welshy. But not for me, sounds like it's right up Berni's street.' Berni nodded in agreement.

'Right you two, we need to be on our way.' Cagney said firmly. 'And just so you know the concert that's on tonight is The Hallé orchestra, playing Elgar's great concerto *Autumnal in Mood*, in case the conversation should go in that direction.' Shauna just looked across at me nonplussed.

'Am I supposed to understand any of that? The only Halle I know is Halle Berry and I'm guessing that's not who you mean?' Fortunately, this was one of the rare moments when Shauna openly laughed at herself, which broke the tension in the room. We all laughed with Shauna and agreed that none of us had a clue about

Elgar's concerto. As the atmosphere lightened, I noticed that although Berni was smiling, her eyes were not. She had been quiet throughout the proceedings. Berni looked smart and well made up, suitably prepared to blend in with fellow concert goers. I approached her and took her to one side, whilst the others chattered light-heartedly.

'Berni is something wrong, I mean more than just this mission? Would you prefer it if I went instead of you? I could wear a hat and a different coat?'

Berni turned to face me, 'It's not the mission Helena, although I do feel slightly anxious, more about containing our little friend's excitement than being kidnapped.' Berni paused. 'It's Brian. I can't feel him. I don't think he's dead but I can't be sure.' Tears began to fill Berni's eyes. This was not the time to continue with this particular conversation. I hugged Berni tightly.

'I'll go instead.'

'That's not your call to make.' Cagney interrupted. 'MI5 makes the decisions and the plan is in motion. Berni I must ask you to come with me.' Berni nodded and turned towards me, she just managed to whisper in my ear.

'Later Helena,' And with that, a tearful Berni and hyped-up Shauna left the hotel. Andy came across to speak to me and I guided him away from Lacey.

'It's Brian isn't it?' I nodded. 'We need some answers now that Berni has picked up danger signals.'

'Berni's instincts are normally spot on Andy. I hate to think of him out there alone and in pain.' Andy linked arms with me and guided me towards to window and the wondrous view of this rapidly developing city.

'You're right Helena, he is out there alone, but he knows that we will do everything we can to get him rescued. Our job is to stay strong, kick-ass, and get Brian back.'

Miss You Like Crazy

Natalie Cole

I miss you like crazy, I miss you like crazy
Ever since you went away
Every hour of every day
I miss you like crazy
I miss you like crazy

19

Chapter

Back at the house, Jenni was not in the best mood. She had never been a morning person and after a troubled sleep, she was feeling anxious. She'd been awake long before her phone alarm had gone off. Jenni could not afford to make any mistakes or wake anyone up. It was 6.30 am and the excuse she would give for going to the corner shop was that she couldn't sleep, which was now true, and that they had run out of milk, which would also shortly be true. Jenni dressed quietly and padded softly down the stairs. She was holding her breath, which she always did in times of stress and which helped nothing. Jenni entered the kitchen, eased open the fridge door, and located the half-empty bottle of milk. She carefully poured the milk down the sink and used water from the kettle to rinse away the evidence. You could never be too careful where Maxim was concerned. Jenni walked slowly toward the door, taking the empty plastic bottle with her to throw in the bin at the shop, thus hopefully avoiding any holes in her story. She grabbed her handbag and then gently eased the door open, before stepping out into the early morning air. It wasn't light yet but the world was just starting to wake up. This was not Jenni's favourite time of day and she could feel her heart pounding as she approached the shop. She tried to slow her pace to avoid any unwanted attention. After turning the corner, she threw the empty milk bottle in the bin and turned around cautiously to check that no one was following her.

Jenni entered the shop. She smiled and nodded at the shopkeeper who she knew had been briefed. He motioned his head towards the stockroom. Jenni took one last look through the shop window, confident that, should she be asked, she could explain her movements easily up to this point. It would be a little harder to explain if she was seen going into the stockroom. The coast seemed to be clear and Jenni knew that the shopkeeper would signal if anything untoward happened. She entered the stockroom and a very nervous Lacey greeted her enthusiastically. He checked that the door was locked and then could not resist a warm hug that turned into an embrace.

'Not here Lacey and not now.' Jenni said calmly, whilst pushing him back, but not before she carefully stroked the side of his face.

'It's been so long and ...'

'I know Lacey, but now isn't the time or the place.' she said as she gave the dingy stockroom the once over.

'Come sit.' Lacey said pulling her behind the shelving towards two upturned crates. 'How are things, Jenni? Do we need to come in and get you and Brian out?'

Jenni paused. 'It's tempting but then we'll never find out any more about *Crytex* or stand a chance at penetrating their business and also their next move. We know so little about their background, their politics and their plans for *Watcher 22*. If you pull us out now, we are no better off than we were before.'

9 5

'But you'd both be alive.' Lacey said, whilst gently stroking her forearm.

'But for how long? If *Crytex* get hold of *Watcher* and the information regarding Barry's rogue trip to the past and they can work it all out, then what will that mean for the rest of us? If history can be altered, we may not even exist. So yes Lacey, my dear friend it is worth the risk. Although Maxim is not afraid of man or beast and would not flinch in taking someone's life.'

'I hear what you're saying, but it doesn't make me feel any better. What's the situation with the Neighbourhood Watch guy?' Jenni explained about Steve's trip to Centreparcs.

'It's a shame that he didn't go for a week. But I think that could be arranged if you think it would help and give you more time?'

'No, I think that would spook Maxim and he might then start to look more closely at the team members, which we definitely do not want. I just need the safe house to be ready, then we can move and put this business behind us.'

How's Brian doing? Berni has picked up some feelings of fear which is to be expected but more worryingly she senses that Brian is in pain, and she's not usually far off the mark.'

'Brian was struck across the head after he tried to alert the Neighbourhood Watch guy by banging on a pipe. But now he's drugged most of the time. Maxim has taken over his 'care' so it's hard to get in and see him. I do check that the food plate comes back empty and as far as I can tell Maxim hasn't hit him again. But as the pressure increases Maxim becomes more unpredictable. I question his loyalty to *Crytex* and his ability to follow instructions.

He may have a hidden agenda or perhaps his loyalties lie elsewhere, he is Russian after all. I know that *Crytex* has a rigid selection process and training programme.' Jenni paused. 'But then again, I got through the very same process, so it's not foolproof.'

'Is there anything else you want us to know? You called this meeting Jenni.'

'Do MI5 know about the new threat with the neighbours? I'm sure that Steve, the Neighbourhood Watch man, saw Carl's army watch. If so this may have blown his cover. Obviously, we have not told Maxim, even Carl is scared of him. The sighting of the watch combined with the noises from the cellar may arouse Mr. Nosey to pay us another visit on his return. This could place his life and the lives of his family in danger. He needs to keep clear.'

'Should he be warned off Jenni?'

'Would that stop a man like Steve or make him more inquisitive? Steve knew how to take orders, but the question is would he follow orders now that he's a civilian? He has a wife and a young family to take care of. Our best bet is the safe house. Once we move, Steve can have all the answers he wants, but not before we go.'

'OK, I will pass your intel on. We are on a very tight time-line. If you haven't moved to the safe house in two days or Maxim starts to get suspicious, then we pull you both out. Agreed?'

Jenni nodded in agreement. Lacey's phone then buzzed, signalling the end of their meeting. Lacey reassured Jenni that she was not alone, surveillance was 24/7 and the team were on standby should she initiate the emergency protocol. He thanked her for the update and gave her one last hug.

'I'll leave first, I'll go out of the back door.'

'Won't that look more suspicious and weren't you meant to be buying some milk?'

'Oh God, yes you're right! Sorry, I'm a bit rattled. They said their goodbyes and

Jenni left the store room holding back tears and longing to return to her old life. The door opened into the back room of the shop, where all the tins of condensed soup and pot noodles were stacked on metal shelves. Jenni picked up some Vim and some Jay cloths to make her visit to the 'back room' appear worthwhile. She went down the steps and into the main shop and just as she opened the door of the fridge to grab the milk, she caught the eye of the shopkeeper. He had a good view out of the front window. As Jenni approached with the plastic milk bottle, she could tell by his face that something was wrong. Jenni looked out of the shop window and that's when she saw him, Maxim. He was leaning against the shop wall, hands in his pockets and kicking some imaginary stones. Maxim had one of his favourite Chupa Chup lollies positioned like a cigarette in the corner of his mouth. Jenni caught Maxim's eye and he nodded in recognition. She paid for the goods and asked the shopkeeper how long Maxim had been there. This was vital information as she had to prepare an accurate storyline. The shopkeeper signalled a five with his hand. Jenni nodded in assent, thanked him, and opened the door to face the interrogation that she knew would come.

Pompeii

Bastille

But if you close your eyes
Does it almost feel like nothing changed at all?
And if you close your eyes
Does it almost feel like you've been here before?
How am I gonna be an optimist about this?
How am I gonna be an optimist about this?

Although Shauna was not renowned for her tact and diplomacy, you could never fault her empathy and compassion. The tough exterior and overconfidence were merely a protective cover that had built up over the years. In the back of the shiny new Range Rover, safely hidden behind the tinted windows, Shauna placed a comforting arm around Berni's shoulder.

'Come on Berni, we can fuckin' do this!'

'So eloquently put as always, my dear.'

'I don't know what that means, but I do know that we have to stay strong to save Brian. If we have to go to this Bridgerton Hall to get more clues, then so be it. I didn't love the TV series, but each to their own. There was quite a hot guy in it though...' Shauna stopped as she realised that Berni was suppressing a giggle. 'What? Was it one of your favourites Berni is that it? Are you a secret Bridgerton fan?'

'That's not it Shauna. 'Berni said smiling 'It's The Bridgewater Hall, not Bridgerton and by the way, I agree with you Regé-Jean Page was more than pleasing to the eye.'

'It wouldn't mind if he pleased me somewhere else...'

'Ladies, if you could just behave yourselves and focus on the job at hand.' Brown was uptight.

'I know what I'd like to get in my hand…'

'Shauna, please! Brown snapped at her. But Shauna had worked her magic and Berni's mood had lifted. She caught Cagney's eye in the rear-view mirror and he winked at her, before adopting his serious face. The Range Rover came to a stop directly outside The Bridgewater Hall. Cagney opened the door and Berni and Shauna stepped out into the bright sunshine which served to light up the magnificent building.

'Wow it's fuckin' amazing!' exclaimed Shauna as they gazed upwards at the mighty building. The structure combined solid concrete with a stainless shell outer shell and this contrasted beautifully with the deep red sandstone walls. The beautiful glass windows and aluminium frame gave it both light and space, it was like a vast sculpture decorating this very urban landscape.

'Truly remarkable!' Berni said as she tried to take it all in.

'Ladies, we do need to move and retrieve the next clue or Brown will be on the case. Berni and Shauna walked slowly toward the entrance and stopped to have their bags searched, a practice that is now seen as standard following the horrors of the Manchester bombing. Cagney could have flashed his credentials but wanted to avoid attracting any unnecessary attention. Once the bag search was complete, they entered the building via the huge glass doors.

On the left of the entrance, there was a lovely cafe with stunning views, but there was no time for a visit today. To the right was the booking desk and cloakroom.

I'll stay here and keep a close watch.' Cagney said. 'You two go to the booking desk.' Shauna and Berni both nodded and joined the queue.

'I bet that's Simon.' Shauna said, signalling her head towards one of the staff serving behind the desk.

'Let's hope so Shauna, as the other assistant is a woman.'

Shauna let out a little snort which gained the attention of some of the other queue members. 'What if we get called to the other desk and we don't get Simon?'

'Then we just ask if we can have a word with him.'

'Won't that look suspicious?' Shauna asked anxiously.

'Let's just see who we get, before fretting about it.'

'Excuse me. I think this may have come out of your purse.' Berni and Shauna turned around to face a rather tall and distinguished-looking gentleman. Berni flushed as the man handed her a slip of paper.

'Shauna just check this for me if you would, I don't have my glasses to hand.'

'Of course your Ladyship.' Shauna said as she presented Berni with a mock curtsy.

'One multi-buy offer - Barbecue chicken and bacon cheese-filled crust pizza..'

'Thank you, Shauna, but I don't think that receipt is mine.' Berni said blushing slightly.

'Iceland Meal in a Bag Cheesy Chicken and Broccoli Pasta. Magnum double raspberry ice cream...'

'Thank you, Shauna. No need to continue, I rarely shop in Iceland.' Berni said as she retrieved the receipt and crumpled it in her hand.

'Pity.' the man said smiling 'as the Magnums were a great choice, the raspberry is my particular favourite.'

Berni looked slightly flushed and her blue eyes shone a little too brightly. This guy was smooth.

Shauna grinned to herself and turned to face the booking desk. She recognised a classic one-liner when she heard it and wanted to give Berni some space. They edged their way to the front of the queue and Shauna was hoping that Simon would serve them. But it was not to be. She grabbed Berni's arm. They were next in line, but it was the rather twitchy female server who beckoned them forward. Berni turned to ask her new-found friend if he would like to go ahead of them, as they had a block of tickets to buy for a work conference. Whether the Richard Gere 'lookie-likie' believed them or not was debatable, but he happily took their place to be served by the twitcher. A few moments later, it was their turn. They approached the desk cautiously, Shauna looking behind them as Berni asked for the programme.

'The programmes are available over by the cloakroom, I'm afraid. Sorry you have wasted your time queuing.'

'You are Simon right?' Shauna said quietly as she leaned toward the glass screen. Simon nodded, looking slightly uncomfortable. He looked down at his badge and then back at Shauna.

'Is there something else I can help you with?' he asked cautiously.

'Look Simon, stop pissing about...'

'What my lovely friend here is trying to say...' Berni interjected. 'is that you may have been expecting us and have something to give us.' Simon still seemed uncertain and his eyebrows drew together in a puzzled frown.

'Just give us the soddin' envelope!' Shauna said loudly, attracting attention from fellow queuers and a raised eyebrow from Handsome Richard as he walked past them after purchasing his tickets. It was a mixture of anger at Shauna's behaviour and then seeing Handsome Richard depart that prompted Berni to become a little more direct.

'Look, Simon, I'd like you to think back, a man called Barry left a package or letter with you, it may have been some time ago. Simon was racking his brains and then he had the light bulb moment.

'Deirdre, I need the key for the cabinet.' he shouted over to the twitcher who immediately located the key and passed it over to him.

'One moment.' he said as he swivelled his chair around, stood up, and then opened the filing cabinet at the back of the office. He knew which drawer it was in and located the brown buff A4 envelope. He locked the cabinet and returned the key to Deirdre. Simon smiled.

'It was some time ago, apologies for the slow recall, I do just have to ask you one security question.' Simon read the question from the orange Post-it note which was stuck on the outside of the envelope.

'Please confirm the name of Barry's solicitor and your key handler from Experenta?'

'That's easy Chadwick and Brown.' Shauna said quickly. 'If you could destroy the Post it Simon that would be great.'

Simon screwed up the Post-it note and threw it away, he then slid the envelope across the counter, gave them a polite nod, and signalled for the next customer to come forward.

Berni and Shauna walked over to the cloakroom area to meet Cagney and get a programme. Handsome Richard was also looking at the programmes. Nothing suspicious about that or was there? Shauna picked up a programme as he approached. Was it her imagination or was he looking at the envelope that Berni had folded in half and was trying to ram into her handbag? Handsome Richard smiled sweetly before leaning across in an attempt to snatch the envelope from Berni. Cagney swooped in and blocked him with his body.

'We leave now, he said guiding them towards the door. The backup team will pick up lover boy. 'Now move!!'

Chain reaction

Diana Ross

You took a mystery and made me want it
You got a pedestal and put me on it
You made me love you out of feeling nothing
Something that you do
And I was there and not dancing with anyone
You took a little, then you took me over
You set your mark on stealing my heart away
Crying, trying, anything for you

21

Chapter

'It's unusual to see you up so early Jenni.' Maxim said without giving her any eye contact. Jenni was already on her guard. Maxim was a well-trained interrogator and it was typical for him to begin with a 'softly softly' approach.

'I couldn't sleep, so I thought that I'd have a brew and that's when I realised that we were out of milk and as it was a beautiful morning and well here I am.'

'Here you are indeed. It's strange, as when I checked last night I was sure that we had enough milk.' Maxim said as he turned to look her straight in the eye.

'I see you have also bought cleaning products. Are you expecting we will need a deep clean soon?' It was Jenni's turn to pause. Maxim's blue eyes seemed to bore into her, with an intensity that chilled her to the core. This was a ruthless killer, any whiff of suspicion and he wouldn't hesitate in killing her and she knew it. Maxim ran his fingers through his matted grey hair which was still wet from his early morning shower. That must have been when he discovered her absence.

'Actually, I thought the kitchen could do with a good clean as we may be leaving for the new safe house soon.' It was a lame explanation and she knew it and so did

Maxim. 'Anything else?' Jenni said, casting him a sideways glance. Maxim paused and this unnerved Jenni more than any targeted questioning would have.

'No nothing more.'

They continued walking in an uncomfortable silence. Jenni could feel her heartbeat banging in her head, a familiar sign of distress. As they approached Steve's house, Maxim began to slow down and then came to an abrupt stop. Again he turned to face her.

'This idiot...' he signalled towards Steve's house with his head, 'should be back from his holiday soon?'

'Two more days I think, I'm hoping we'll have gone before he comes back.'

'I'm sure you are, but *Crytex* has not informed me yet.'

'That's a shame, but I feel confident that Carl and I curtailed his interest after that unfortunate incident.'

'I hope you are right Jenni. It would be 'unfortunate' for Steve if he became a problem. The mission is more important than this neighbour and I won't put up with any unwanted attention. Do I make myself clear?'

'Crystal clear Maxim. And while I'm here I did promise to check on his property while he's away, so if you don't mind?'

'Would you like me to join you?' Maxim asked, his expression had not changed. It was a difficult call for Jenni, if she said no it may arouse suspicion, but if she said yes it would allow him to continue observing and questioning her.

'I'm only going to give it the once over. But come along if you want.'

Maxim paused again before answering.

'I think I'll wait here, in case you find anything. Give me the shopping.'

It was a direct order rather than a request. Was he on to her? He suspected something. Thank God she had not brought along any of the MI5 alert stickers or she'd be done for. She had hidden them in her room. They were safe for now, or so she hoped. Jenni checked the front of Steve's house, everything looked secure. She pushed a random flyer through the letterbox, as half of it was hanging out and Steve would surely pick up on this as a clear indicator that the house was unoccupied. Next, she sidled down the passageway between the houses and opened the rusty wrought iron gate. Jenni was surprised that it wasn't padlocked. She left the gate open as a sign to Maxim that she wasn't hiding anything. She dutifully checked the shed and it was still safely padlocked. Everything seemed secure and there was no sign that anything had been tampered with. As she walked across the garden towards the patio doors, Jenni happened to glance across at their own house and that's when she noticed. She froze, just for a second, her heart rate quickened and she felt slightly nauseous.

As Jenni slept in the bedroom at the back of the house, her eyes were drawn to her bedroom window. She was also 100 percent certain that she had left the curtains closed when she sneaked out of the house in the early hours. Someone had drawn back the curtains. Jenni always thought that at some point Maxim would search her room, she just thought he would do it more carefully. This was a bad omen, if Maxim could not be bothered to do the search covertly, it meant that he had nothing to hide and no one of significance to answer to.

Thankfully, she had left the only piece of incriminating evidence, the MI5 alert sticker safely hidden. If Maxim had found anything she felt sure that he would act before they returned to the house. She would be eliminated, of that she was certain. Jenni jolted herself into the present day and tried to carry on as normal.

The patio doors at Neighbourhood Watch guy's house were, of course, secure and as was the back door. She could delay it no longer, she had to return to Maxim. He was an expert at picking up signals and reading people, even the slightest flicker of self-doubt would put him on the attack. Jenni thought back to her training and pushed her thumb hard into the fleshy part of her hand between her thumb and forefinger. She then repeated this on the other hand, took two deep breaths, and stopped herself from biting her lip. It was hard to control her anxiety but she mustn't slip now, Maxim may not have found the stickers but she could blow her cover just by losing her cool. She forced herself to walk slowly up the passageway, back toward Maxim. He was sitting on the low garden wall with his back to her.

'All is good?' he said as he turned to face her.

'Yes, all secure.' Jenni said trying to keep her voice even.

'We go back now, there's something I want to show you.' He indicated his head towards the house. Jenni's heart thumped loudly in her chest, it was so loud that she was sure that Maxim would hear it. They walked in silence and that's when it happened. Carl burst out through the front door.

'Where have you been? There's been a message for you Maxim on the burner, in code of course, but it seems urgent!' Maxim thrust the shopping bag towards Jenni and pushed passed Carl as he headed inside. Carl looked across at Jenni guiding her gently towards the kitchen.

'Ah you got milk.' he said loudly. 'Good job. I'll get the kettle on.' As he ran the water, Carl leaned over and whispered in Jenni's ear.

'What the hell is going on? Your room's been tossed. Ripped apart. I hope you know what you're doing Jenni!'

Before she could respond, Maxim barged into the kitchen.

'Now we pack.' he paused then looked over at Jenni. 'All of us. The safe house is ready, we go now. Jenni I will speak with you later.' and with that Maxim stormed out of the room.

'What the fuck is going on? Where have you been and...' but before he could finish Maxim shouted for Carl to help him move Brian. Jenni flicked off the kettle and took a deep breath. Steve and his family would now be safe, but her survival had been jeopardised. She left the kitchen and ran up the stairs. She entered her bedroom which had been roughly searched by Maxim. The mattress was on its side, the sheets had been ripped off. Jenni closed the door behind her, moved the bedding to one side and edged the mattress back onto the bed. She had tucked the 3 remaining stickers behind the handle on the side of the mattress. These were her only hope of rescue if things went wrong. But were they still there or had Maxim found them?

Boulevard of Broken Dreams

Green Day

I walk a lonely road
The only one that I have ever known
Don't know where it goes
But it's home to me, and I walk alone

22

Chapter

'It's so humiliating.' Berni said when they were safely on the move in the Range Rover.

'You're not the first to be caught in a honey trap Berni and you won't be the last.' Brown said somewhat smugly.

'And he was flippin' hot was Handsome Richard, no doubt about it.' Shauna added, trying to reassure Berni.

'He was a convincing player Berni, but we were watching him.'

'You could have warned her Cagney!'

'We were trying to keep things low key, remember, and you were never in any direct danger. Just remember that we always monitor all of you, all of the time.'

'Look there's no harm done. We have what we came for and now we can solve the second clue.' Brown said pragmatically, before relenting a little. 'Are you feeling a little calmer now Berni?' It was one of Brown's rhetorical questions. 'Good, well things have moved on a little. There is nothing to be concerned about, but we won't be returning to the Hilton. Don't panic Shauna, all your belongings were packed up by Helena and yours too Berni. Our cover has been blown and we have been there for a while, a move was already on the cards. Helena and Andy are waiting for us in the new hotel.'

'Where are we off to now Brown?' Before he could answer, his phone rang and he turned away to take the call. Cagney caught Shauna's eye in the rear-view mirror and nodded reassuringly. Shauna nodded back before looking out of the window, they were heading towards Piccadilly station. Berni was still recovering from the shock, but we all knew that embarrassment was harder to handle.

It was a quick journey and before they knew it they were once again stepping out in the bright sunshine.

'Bloody hell!! What's this hotel meant to be about? It looks like a giant game of Jenga!'

'Funny you should say that Shauna, I managed to find some info and you are bang on the money. This is the Leonardo Hotel, Manchester. Thirteen stories of white concrete blocks, incorporating planted balconies, it was inspired by Jenga blocks,' he paused and pointed at Shauna in recognition. 'And also by the vertical forest tower blocks in Milan, which you may have seen on TV.' Shauna shook her head.

'I have seen the forest towers on TV Cagney. They are tower blocks with plants and shrubs growing on the outside of the buildings. What you will love Shauna is that they employ "Flying Gardeners" a specialised team of climbers who, using mountaineering techniques and descend from the roof of the buildings once a year to carry out pruning and checking the plants.' Berni was back in the game.

'Wow!!! That's ace! Are they going to grow all that stuff down this building then?'

'I doubt it, not on that scale anyway.' Cagney said abruptly as he guided them towards the entrance.

They entered the hotel and were immediately whisked to their suite, forgoing the usual formalities. The rest of the team were waiting for them in a meeting room that had full-length patio-style windows and long white cushioned banquettes that reflected the style of the square Jenga blocks. It was clean and light, and lush green plants adorned the white walls. They had the usual group hug. White oblong tables and chairs were brought in, along with the usual drinks and snacks. Brown appeared, accompanied by Lacey and the meeting began.

'It was difficult not to smile when we were told about Handsome Richard.' Andy said, controlling his mirth out of courtesy. I patted Berni's arm as a mark of solidarity and reassurance.

'Said fellow is now in custody and being questioned by MI5, so he may not be as handsome by the end of the day.' Shauna broke the silence first and soon everyone was chatting light-heartedly. Brown soon stepped in.

'If we could just focus.... Thank you.' Brown said loudly 'We now have the second clue, successfully procured by Cagney, Berni and Shauna.' a light round of applause followed, but was immediately silenced by Brown.

'Once we have Brian back amongst us there will be plenty of time to celebrate. If you could do the honours Cagney, as you secured the envelope.'

Cagney wasted no time in ripping the envelope open and a familiar piece of pale blue Basildon Bond paper flew across the table. Andy retrieved it.

'Spill the beans Welshy!' Shauna said impatiently. 'We want to know what all that palaver was in aid of.'

'Well, what are you waiting for man? Read it out!' Cagney showed just the slightest flicker of annoyance and a narrowing of the eyes, but he'd been trained well and there were bigger fish to fry.

'The second clue.' Andy stopped abruptly. 'I think the next sentence is Latin and…'

'Yes yes, we understand. Hand it to me.' Brown whisked the sheet from Andy's hands and wasted no time in reading the clue aloud.

'Hoc est corpus meum.' Brown paused and seemed to struggle with the translation. 'This is my body? Does anyone else know Latin?'

Berni responded. 'You are correct Brown, it's from the Latin blessing from the Catholic mass.'

'So what the …'

'Shauna, if you could just be patient.' Brown said quite sternly. Shauna begin kicking the side of the white padded banquette and glowering at Brown, danger signs were a go.

'Maybe Barry has hidden the clue in his body, has he been…'

'Indeed he has Shauna. The service was held yesterday, it was the wishes of the family. And before you ask he was cremated, so there is no body to search.'

'I think we are going to have to do some research on this one. Clever old fox that Barry is turning out to be.' None of us were allowed to have phones. Lacey produced a tablet and accessed the internet within seconds. Brown handed him the note.

'Well, you are correct with the translation. But I don't think bodies are involved. Hoc est corpus meum does mean 'This is my body'. It says here that 'Hocus Pocus' was a name people more commonly used. It is a popular perversion of the Latin blessing from the Catholic mass.'

'Is this 'Hocus Pocus' a computer game?' Berni asked.

'I only know the film with Bette Midler and Sarah Jessica Parker in. But what is the connection?'

'Piece of piss.' Shauna announced loudly as she found the entertainment programme from The Bridgewater Hall.

'I thought I'd seen the name somewhere. Ah, here it is.' Shauna said as she thumbed through the programme. 'The iconic Disney film 'Hocus Pocus' in concert on Monday 24th October. We have our date!'

'That's excellent. Well done all and good work young Shauna.' Brown said giving one of his half smiles. Shauna disguised a shudder as he turned to leave.

'Get some rest! We go again at midday. And before any of you complain, we have escalated the programme as we are concerned about Brian's welfare. I can say no more.' Brown then left the room, we secretly thought that he enjoyed a dramatic exit.

'He's right, Brian is struggling, I can tell.' Berni went quiet. I always knew when to jump in.

'Let's unpack, rest up and go back out there tomorrow.'

Witchcraft

Frank Sinatra

Those fingers in my hair
That sly come hither stare
That strips my conscience bare
It's witchcraft

23

Chapter

In another lifetime, the remote cottage that Maxim drove them to would have been idyllic. Nestled amongst the trees, in the heart of the countryside, the cottage was almost hidden from view. A long winding gravel drive led to a perfect rural location. The journey had been uneventful. Jenni had only managed to catch a glimpse of Brian as he was lifted into the boot of the Range Rover swaddled in blankets. His pale face was only visible for a moment as it caught the sunshine, but his eyes were closed, more drugs had been administered. It had only taken thirty-five minutes to reach the cottage, who would have known that this was so close to the city? There would be no signalling opportunity for Jenni from here and no local shop to meet up with Lacey. Jenni prayed that he had placed a tracker on the car, as MI5 now knew they were about to relocate. She was desperately hoping that there would be a sign, a signal, or some sort of message from MI5, maybe not straight away but once the dust had settled. Jenni shuddered as the car crunched to a sudden stop. Maxim had parked at the side of the cottage, the Range Rover would be hidden by a wooden lean-to, which wasn't visible from the driveway. Maxim was a cunning and

117

powerful opponent and with the backing of *Crytex* and their multi-million-pound budget, he was a powerful asset.

Within hours they had settled into the rural retreat Jenni had been observant on the journey and calculated that the nearest farm was at least fifteen minutes by car, with no easy escape should they need it. Brian had been taken to one of the outhouses, there would be no nosy neighbours to hear any calls for help here. Perhaps Maxim would drug him a little less.

'Jenni, stop the daydreaming and bring the batteries over to me.' Maxim instructed. Everyone sat at the round pine table, the sturdy chairs were made comfortable with red checked cushions, tied on with red sashes. The pretty red check curtains were tied with the same sashes. There was an AGA cooker of course and a pine Welsh dresser laden with china plates and cups and saucers. It was cosy and comfortable and the views from the window were breathtaking.

'Are you deaf! Jenni get the batteries.' Carl nudged her into the moment and flashed her a quizzical look. Jenni rose from the table and rummaged through the Tesco carrier bag. She found the rechargeable battery packs and dropped them onto the table in front of Maxim. He glared at her and was about to speak when Carl, sensing trouble, intervened.

'Coffee and sandwiches, that's what we need. Lend a hand Jenni.' Jenni felt herself being guided over to the pine kitchen top, as Carl turned her to one side and shook his head in warning. Jenni felt that he had her back. She took a deep breath and nodded her assent. The shrill whistle of the kettle cut through the air, drinks were made and some sort of peace had been restored. Maxim's focus had shifted as he and Lars ripped open the packaging like excited school boys and then Maxim excitedly showed off the long-range walkie-talkies. Jenni had seen them before on one of the training missions she'd attended. They have no data limits and are particularly useful in remote places where cell phone reception is unreliable. But more importantly, this particular make of walkie-talkie had a thirty-five mile range. Within minutes Lars and Maxim had them working and the sound and reception were both excellent. Perfect considering the location of the cottage. Maxim made Lars stand outside the outhouse where Brian was being held. Again the reception was perfect. Jenni knew that Maxim also had a burner phone which never left his pocket, but the burner may be the only way she could make contact if things took a bad turn.

'There will be a message tonight.' Maxim interrupted her train of thought. We may need to 'invite' Brian to make another recording just to give his friends an incentive to cooperate. *Crytex* is not happy with the clues from the team and feels that some information is begin withheld.'

'Time to play with our catch, make him squeal a little. He could do with some exercise, maybe a cat and mouse hey Maxim.' Maxim smiled at Lars who looked happy for once, for all the wrong reasons.

'I'm in charge here Lars and for now, he stays alive and in a good enough condition to make the recordings. After that…well we shall see my friend. I know how you like the chase, it may be possible.'

Jenni shuddered and even Carl looked away. All of their 'games' involved violence, cruelty and bloodshed.

Lars and Maxim attached the new walkie-talkies to their belts. Jenni and Carl didn't even bother to ask if they could have one, it was clear who the leaders in this group were.

'We're going to play with our little friend. You two stay here and do whatever it is you do. I don't know why *Crytex* sent you, but for now, you can play house.'

Jenni was relieved when they left the kitchen but frightened for Brian. She still wasn't convinced that she could trust Carl. True he had backed her up when the Neighbourhood Watch guy, Steve, was interfering. Also true that he was no fan of torture or bloodshed. Jenni knew that she would be taking a great risk if she blew her cover, but she needed to test the water. and this was a rare opportunity.

'So Carl, shall we cook? It doesn't look as though we'll be involved with much else?'

'I guess we can. I think things are getting serious with our friend.' he indicated his head toward the outhouse. 'I want no part of it if they torture him or kill him. I wasn't sent here for that.'

Jenni saw her chance. 'Why were you sent here Carl?'

'I represent *Crytex* of course, just as you do.'

Jenni knew a brush-off when she heard it.

'No really Carl, what is your role here?'

'To keep the peace mainly and try to lower the tempo of the violence and restrain brutality where possible. That's all I can say. Maxim was brought in for his aggressive nature and ability to kidnap and extort information. Lars is just his monkey. *Crytex* wants the information from the group who search for the keys and the clues. Brian is innocent in all this. I was sent to

120

observe and be the voice of reason. Now I have got to know Maxim, I see there's little chance of that. I've said enough.' Carl bit his lip as he began slicing the potatoes that Jenni had just peeled.

'You're a kind of military negotiator then?'

'Enough. Now we talk about you. You're not like them and they know it. But I know you passed the *Crytex* induction. What are you doing here Jenni and who are you working with?'

Fortunately, the door slammed shut as Maxim and Lars came back into the cottage and Jenni didn't have time to answer.

'Brian is no fun.' Lars said kicking the chair back with his foot. 'He gave us exactly what we wanted.'

'I did let you rough him up a little.' Maxim said trying to appease him.

'It's not got the fun of the chase Max and you know this.'

'Bide your time Lars, your too impatient. There are six clues and we only have three. Your turn will come.'

Run for home

Lindisfarne

Run for home, run as fast as I can
Whoa, running man, running for home
Run for home, run as fast as I can
Whoa, running man, running for home

24

Chapter

'There's no rest for the wicked.' Shauna grumbled as the communal alarm bell rang angrily through the suite of rooms.

'You're just disappointed that it's not like Enid Blyton's Chalet School.' I said smiling.

'I don't know what the fuck that is.' Shauna said snappily as she pulled on her jeans. 'Didn't she write *Noddy*?'

'Very good Shauna, especially at this time of the morning.' Berni said pleasantly. Shauna rounded on her, ready to launch one of her infamous verbal torpedoes. Fortunately, Lacey interrupted, by knocking loudly on the door and the moment was lost.

Brown was already up and running as we entered the meeting room. The usual fare of coffee tea and light breakfast snacks adorned the table.

'Grab a drink etcetera and then we will begin.' Brown demanded. He had prepared a power-point, which was ready to be projected onto a screen. We obeyed quietly and Andy entered the room, recently showered and doused in Lynx Africa. I caught Andy's eye and raised a questioning eyebrow, all the while hoping that Shauna didn't get a whiff, too late.

'What the fuck Andy! You smell like a whore's...' Luckily we'll never know the complete simile, as Brown was in no mood for shenanigans.

'Let's have some quiet. Do I need to remind you again that Brian's life is in danger? Today I can share some of the Intel cleared by MI5, which is obviously for your eyes and ears only.'

'Like there's anyone we can tell....'

'Choose your moments for flippancy carefully Shauna, I can assure you that this is not one of them.' Shauna flushed and the 'tell', of looking down at her feet in anger, soon came into play. I just hoped she could contain herself for the rest of the meeting. Cagney dimmed the lights and Brown began.

'Brian is alive, but possibly not in the best of health. We have been told by a reliable source that he is being drugged following a failed escape attempt. The group holding him is known to MI5. These are ruthless mercenaries who will not hesitate in killing Brian if they don't get what they want. At present, they are struggling with the 'Hocus Pocus' clue as it is so obscure. Inevitably, we will have to give them the answer, to prevent any further harm coming to Brian. This gives us a small window of time to get ahead of the game.' Andy raised his hand. Brown looked slightly irritated to have his flow stemmed, but allowed the question.

'How do they know? About the 'Hocus Pocus' clue. I memorised the clue when I was at the bank and then Simon gave us the envelope which Handsome Richard tried to steal, but thanks to Cagney they never got it. So my question to you is, how do they know anything about that clue?' Brown sighed. 'Come on Brown! We're the ones taking all the risks on the ground here. And it sounds like poor Brian never gets to see the light of day. Any one of us could be next! So I think we deserve some answers. It's our lives on the line, not yours, not the staff at *Experenta* or the MI5 officers! It's us five.' Andy gesticulated towards the remaining group members 'One of whom has already been captured.' We all banged the table in support and out of the corner of my eye Cagney and Lacey displayed their discomfort with their silence.

'Quieten down please.' Brown said, clearly irked. 'Very well. You are correct Andy. We did outfox them with the clue. However, the kidnappers don't play fair or by the book and their trump card is Brian and the leverage this creates. The powers that be have agreed that Clue 2 should be passed to the kidnappers. The risk to life is simply too high.' I could tell that Shauna was about to blow.

'So the bastards weren't 'struggling' with the 'Hocus Pocus' clue at all, you said that to mislead us. You lot just gave it to them, they asked and you caved in! Now they know when the soddin' meeting will take place and the date?'

Brown paused, allowing Cagney to speak up.

'The 'bastards' do know Shauna, we had to trade that for Brian's life. Just as we would have done to save your life or any member of this team! It would serve you well to remember that!'

'That's enough Cagney.' Brown said firmly. 'We had no choice, end of story. We lost the clue but that was the price of keeping Brian alive. His life is in our hands. We are fortunate enough to have MI5 protecting us.' Brown paused. Lacey, could you debrief? Brown looked jaded and we needed to remember that he wasn't working for MI5 and he didn't have their specialist training. It was all taking its toll on him as well as us. Lacey stood up and Cagney changed the screen.

'Things will speed up from now on, the Intel we have received has exposed the heightened danger not just for Brian but also for our Informant.' Berni looked across at me, a glint of a tear in her eye. But this was no time to falter, our friend was relying on us.

The screen saver was clicked off and a photograph of Manchester Cathedral adorned the screen. Lacey flashed a smile across to me before reverting to his serious face,

'This is where the next clue will be located. And before you ask, we know this as Clue 3 was written into the Will to throw the bad guys off the scent. Barry merely alluded to Helena's great great Uncle and added a strange clue - *read your bible well.*'

'Who told you though? Only the group knows about this.' Helena said, looking confused.

'Andy filled in the gaps for us and told us about your newly found family connection to the renowned Bishop of Manchester, Bishop Fraser. Barry knew of it and simply left a written reference to your connection with him and then the cathedral which immediately gave us the location. Helena and Andy, get your coats. We will take you to the Bishop's chapel, you will need to take photographs of everything in there and return to decipher the clue using the code Barry left. This is our chance to get ahead as the kidnappers will be watching the bank.'

'Let's go!' Brown said with some urgency. Within minutes we were back in the Range Rover, weaving our way through the traffic. It was then that I heard it, it was faint but easily recognisable. There was an unmistakable chuckle before the music became louder. This was my absolute favourite version of this song and someone knew it. Flint was still with us and still enjoying himself, but I was grateful to hear this song in light of things to come.

Hallelujah

Celine Dion & The Canadian Tenors

Now I've heard there was a secret chord
That David played, and it pleased the Lord
But you don't really care for music, do you?
It goes like this, the fourth, the fifth
The minor falls, the major lifts
The baffled king composing Hallelujah

Hallelujah, Hallelujah
Hallelujah, Hallelujah

25

The first night at the cottage was uneventful. Everyone was tired and it was too soon to try and get a message to MI5. Brian had survived last night's ordeal, they would leave him alone if he proved to be enough leverage. But Jenni knew that she needed to get more information about Crytex, that was the real reason she had been placed with this group of mercenaries. She would build up her relationship with Carl first. Maxim was a dangerous man and he already thought she was irrelevant. Jenni would have to be very careful, he suspected her motives and this put her in a vulnerable position.

Jenni woke early, it was only 6.30 am and fortunately, the house seemed quiet. She grabbed her toiletries bag and headed for the bathroom hoping for a long, relaxing, and uninterrupted shower. It was then that she heard it, before she had even closed the bathroom door. The throbbing sound was familiar and it was getting louder. It was too quiet to be a helicopter she thought before realising exactly what it was, a drone. Oh God, what if Maxim heard it and it was one of MI5's? He was already suspicious of her. Surely MI5 wouldn't risk it. Of course, it could be a Crytex drone just checking up on them. Either way, she didn't need the tension in the cottage to ramp up, Maxim and Lars were volatile enough without any provocation. All she had wanted was some quiet time and a lovely long shower. Jenni closed the bathroom door as quietly as she could. She padded across the bare varnished floorboards, hoping they didn't creak, and then eased open the bathroom window. The sound of the thudding blades of the drone became louder. The red flashing light helped her to locate it as it flew directly over the cottage.

Jenni's thoughts went into overdrive. If MI5 had placed a tracker on the car and Maxim found it, the consequences for not only her but also Brian could be fatal. She closed the window and made a snap decision. Action was needed if she was to protect their precarious position. She opened the bathroom door and checked for any sounds of activity. The coast seemed clear and no one had emerged from their rooms as yet. Without further ado, Jenni padded softly down the stairs and unlocked the solid oak front door, fortunately, the key had been left in the lock. The combination of the remote location and so many weapons being inside the house meant that Maxim had not removed the key, for now at least. Jenni needed to check the Range Rover for a tracker, she didn't have the key but was praying that it would be an external device. It was a 50/50 chance, she knew the odds from her training. Jenni took a deep breath as she walked across the courtyard to the side of the cottage. Time was of the essence. Her heart was pounding as she approached the Range Rover. As she had no access to the vehicle she began by checking underneath, but there was no sign of a tracker. Surely they would have attached it outside the vehicle as it would have been a lot simpler and quicker. She hurriedly checked the front bumper. Nothing. Time was running out. Jenni made her way to the rear bumper, all her senses were on high alert. She positioned herself on the damp gravel and felt up inside the bumper. She had no flash light and limited visibility, so it was all done by touch. Nothing. She moved to the other side of the vehicle and repeated the process and that was when she found it. She felt the edge of the plastic box, no more than two inches long, and gently pulled it away from the inside of the bumper and got herself upright. Luckily, she had pockets in her towelling dressing gown and she hurriedly secreted the tracker into the deep pocket. Jenni was about to issue a well-deserved sigh of relief, when a very lively Welsh collie almost took her feet from under her. Jenni loved dogs and managed to calm the high-spirited young sheepdog and grab his collar. It was then that the oak front door was yanked open and a bleary-eyed Maxim glared at her. Lars was lurking in the background, hopping from one foot to the other, eager for excitement.

'What the fuck Jenni?' he said, almost sneering. There was a dangerous glint of suppressed hatred in his eyes, which due to his grogginess he had failed to conceal.

'What's she doing outside Maxim, what's she up to?' Lars asked gleefully, hoping for the worst. Jenni gritted her teeth and tried to make her face look neutral before shooting him a look of total disdain. It was lost on Lars, he was too caught up in the moment. Jenni was praying that Carl would show up and soon. Fortunately, before anyone could decide on Jenni's fate, there was a welcome interruption.

'Meg you little sod! Come by.' Meg lowered her tail and all frivolity stopped. There was a spate of whistling and I let go of Meg who dutifully returned to her master. He grabbed Meg by her collar and approached the very odd group.

'Toby Turner. Pleased to meet you. I wondered who had taken the cottage on.' Toby stretched out his free hand to me and then to Maxim. Lars had crawled back under the stone he had emerged from. 'Sorry about Meg, She's young, and lacks control, but in time…'

'Toby. You are on our property because…'

'Ah, apologies. We were on our way to the top pasture when Meg bolted. She used to know the previous tenants, they gave her treats and…'

'There are no treats here now. We came here for privacy, my wife and I.' On cue, Maxim put his arm around me and I tried not to recoil.

'She's been ill you see. Needs peace and quiet. So if you could…'

'Yes, yes of course.' Toby said a little unconvincingly. 'If you do ever need help or there's an emergency I'm only over that hill.' he said pointing over to the left. They hadn't driven any further down the road on their way to the cottage, so Jenni had assumed the nearest sign of life could be miles away. This was excellent news Jenni thought to herself, carefully keeping her face completely straight. Maxim pushed Jenni towards the door. 'We don't need any 'help' or interference Toby. That's why we came here. So again if I could ask you to leave.'

Toby threaded a rope through Meg's collar and before turning to leave, he gave Jenni one last glance.

'I hope you're soon feeling better... erm sorry I didn't catch your name?'

'She's cold out here, my wife, we'll be going in.' Maxim tightened his grip and guided Jenni into the doorway.

'Sorry for the intrusion. Toby said rather curtly. 'I'll be on my way. The offer still stands though if you need anything.'

'We won't.' Maxim snapped back. 'It's privacy we need.' Jenni managed to catch Toby's eye just for a second. She just couldn't tell if he was a real farmer or an agent, CIA maybe. But if she had thought that, then Maxim definitely would. Either way, it was a relief to know that there was a neighbour, albeit over the next hill.

Once the oak door had been closed and locked. Maxim peered through the small glass pane in the oak door, checking that Toby had left. Once he was satisfied, he pulled the little red checked curtain across the small window in the door and then pushed her roughly against the wall.

'What the fuck are you playing at Jenni?' Jenni knew when to keep quiet and pray for distraction or some sort of intervention and yet again lady luck smiled upon her as Carl bounded down the stairs before Maxim could continue.

'Hey, hey what is going on here? Are you alright Jenni?'

'She's alright! But I caught her outside and then this farmer arrived with his pesky dog. Just what we don't need. We are meant to have zero contact with outsiders. Lars go and check if that fuckin' farmer has definitely gone and see to Brian while you're at it. Jenni, in the kitchen now!' Jenni was pushed roughly into the kitchen, Carl forced his way past Maxim and sat down at the table.

'I don't remember asking you to join us!' Maxim said glaring at Carl.

'That's because you didn't! But as I am part of this group, taking the same risks as you, I think I'll stay.' Carl said and Maxim paused for a moment.

'So be it. You make the drinks. And you,' he pointed to Jenni, 'have some explaining to do.'

Brave

Sarah Bareilles

You can be amazing
You can turn a phrase into a weapon or a drug
You can be the outcast
Or be the backlash of somebody's lack of love

26

Chapter

'Well Helena, your distant relative Bishop Fraser certainly made a difference to Manchester. He set up a Board of Education and Manchester Grammar School for Boys, one of the finest schools in the country even today. He also played a part in establishing Owen's College which eventually morphed into the University of Manchester.'

'Wow, that is amazing! Don't you work there Helena, with students at the Uni?'

'I do Andy and I love it.'

'There's another thing that made me think of you Helena.' Brown said, smiling.

'Bishop Fraser's statue stands at the north end of Albert Square looking towards the Cathedral. Local legend has it that he faces away from the Town Hall because he hated the design and wouldn't have wanted his statue to spend the rest of time looking at it! He also won the respect of many after rejecting the comfortable bishop's residence, instead preferring to live in the city centre so he could be closer to the people.'

'What a character! I wish I could have met him. But I'm still grateful that after years of research, we have finally established the family connection. Our bishop had humble beginnings, perhaps education and success proved too much for the family and separated him from the others, but he's part of our family now.'

'Bloody marvellous! He sounds like a great character! And what a cathedral!' Andy said as we pulled up outside the remarkable building. The medieval tower and high clerestory windows showcase the Perpendicular Gothic at its finest. It had been restored and extended in the Victorian period, and again following bomb damage during World War II. Manchester Cathedral is one of fifteen Grade I listed buildings in Manchester and is a glorious spectacle.

We enter the cathedral and admire the nave roof supported by pink marble pillars topped with angels. The majestic arches frame the beautiful stained glass windows. Such a majestic cathedral with imposing arches and ornate details everywhere you look. I was a little overwhelmed until Andy reminded me why we were there.

'Come on Helena, you daydreamer. We need to find your bishop's chapel. Barry sure did go to a lot of trouble over these clues.'

Fortunately, it isn't hard to find Bishop Fraser's chapel as there is a bust of him outside the entrance and luckily the chapel is empty, Andy and I enter and it is lovely. My eyes are immediately drawn to the tomb effigy, which is the sculpted figure of Bishop Fraser, apparently it represents him in a state of 'eternal repose' awaiting resurrection. I know this because I asked Lacey to do a little digging before we set off. The 'People's Bishop' looked at peace. No peace for us though. The stained glass window looks very modern and there is an accompanying frieze on a wooden stand and an open book in front of it. Before I could investigate further, Andy broke my train of thought.

'Helena look at this.' Andy said, whilst tugging at my sleeve and turning me towards the adjacent wall. Just above a wooden bench, there is a plaque that Andy was reading avidly.

'I'll get Brown. We will need a photo. I don't think we can analyse it here and...'

'You are correct Helena, on both counts.' Brown interrupted, clearly in a hurry as he entered the chapel. 'Time is of the essence. If you would stand to one side Andy.' Brown said as he gently pushed Andy. He quickly took the photograph and several others. 'We have to move and now! Lacey thinks we may have company.' We needed no further prompting and within minutes we were back in the Range Rover speeding back to the hotel.

It was good to be reunited with Berni and Shauna. Ever since Brian went missing. We all valued the bonds of our friendship even more.

'About fuckin' time...' Shauna was never one to dress things up.

'Yes yes, now if we could all sit around the table. Cagney, could you work your magic and get the script up on the big screen for us all to see? Helena, you can do the honours.' Brown nodded over to me and sat back in his chair.

'Right OK then.' I said before taking a deep breath. 'In Bishop Fraser's chapel, there is a plaque which we think may be significant in helping us with the third clue. It reads:

To the beloved memory of James Fraser D.D. Bishop of Manchester, 1870 to 1885. A man of singular gifts both of nature and of the Spirit. Brave, true, devout, diligent, in Labours unwearied. He won all hearts by opening to them his own and so administered this Great Diocese as to prove yet once more that the people know the voice of a Good Shepherd and will follow where he leads. This Chapel has been erected by his Devoted Widow May 1887.'

Everyone closely followed the words on the screen as I read them out. There was a brief silence, broken by Berni.

'You must be so proud Helena, of your bishop, he sounds like a wonderful man and so well-liked and respected' I couldn't pretend that I wasn't proud. I know he is only a distant relative but he was the People's Bishop.'

'I love the line - the people know the voice of a good shepherd and will follow where he leads.'

'I agree Helena and I think there lies the clue, 'follow where he leads'.'

'I got kicked out of Sunday School for fuckin' swearing, so I won't be leading you anywhere.' Shauna stated bluntly. 'But anything to do with sheep would be Andy's domain.' she said whilst suppressing a giggle. Andy leaned across the table, waiving his finger, whilst smiling good-naturedly.

'Enough.' Brown said sternly. Lacey, will you look up the reference for the good shepherd, I think it's Psalm 23.' Lacey obliged and quickly located the reference.

'It's in John 10:11. I think we may just have found the meeting time!'

'That's fantastic!' Andy said, thumping his fist down on the table. 'Now we know where and when…'

'Hang on a minute, how do we know if it's morning or night.' Cagney asked cautiously.

'We don't know and we need to, especially as we don't want to get cut off by the tide on the Holy Island of Lindisfarne.'

'Not with these nut jobs chasing us, we don't.'

'Was there nothing else written into the will Brown, perhaps a symbol that may have resembled a squiggle?' Berni asked quietly.

'Checking now, as you speak.' Brown said a little testily. Lacey brought the document onto the screen. 'There isn't much to go on, it just refers to your great great Uncle, unnamed and the words read your bible well.'

'Hang on a flippin' minute.' Shauna said excitedly. 'Lacey make that full stop bigger, much bigger!' Lacey obeyed, Shauna could be very forceful when the mood was on her. Once the font was taken up to 72, it suddenly became clear. It wasn't a full stop, it was a star.

'Bob's your uncle! It's at night time. Looks like we're in for an all-nighter. Well done Shauna! Bloody amazin'. How did you guess?'

'I just thought of what a weird devil Barry was and how he likes to hide things and there we have it.'

'Good job.' Brown admitted begrudgingly. 'Although a night-time operation will complicate things. But at least we know the time and for now, Crytex does not. Get some rest it's an early start for Clue 4. I'll say no more at this stage, but set your alarms for 7.30 am.' Brown left the room and we all gathered together, our group was strong but we knew that there were harder tests to come. We have our night-time group hug and cling to the fact that we are doing the very best we can to save Brian.

Stand By Me

Ben E King

When the night has come
And the land is dark
And the moon is the only light we'll see
No, I won't be afraid
Oh, I won't be afraid
Just as long as you stand
Stand by me

27

Chapter

Maxim glared at Jenni across the pine table, which was covered with a deceptively cheerful, red-checked tablecloth. Jenni noticed that just before Maxim got angry or became violent, his lip curled showing his broken front teeth. She avoided his gaze, still unsure if Maxim had heard the drone. Should she just omit it from her account and pray he would buy the story about Meg the sheepdog? Jenni knew how important the next five minutes could be. Maxim would want a good explanation and he was well-trained at sniffing out bullshit.

'So why were you outside the cottage so early this morning? Just tell me!' Maxim's voice was laced with threat. Jenni tried not to squirm on the pine kitchen chair.

'I don't like your tone.' she said, realising that the volume of her voice was louder than she'd intended. Thankfully, Carl approached with three matching red and white polka dot mugs of steaming hot coffee. He gave Jenni a sideways glance, which felt to her like a warning. Maybe Carl was one of the good guys? But Jenni needed to focus on saving her own skin. Maxim slammed his gun down on the table.

'Enough of these games. You realise what is at stake here! If you fuck with me, you won't do it again. I just don't trust you Jenni, always wandering around at the dawn of the day when no one is up. The same goes for you Carl! Are you working together? Is that it?' Maxim picked up the gun and spun the barrel towards Carl. 'There is something off about you two. And don't give me the drivel about the Crytex screening tests and half-arsed training as a reason why I should. Any half-decent boy scout could get through that!' Maxim turned back towards Jenni and leaned in towards her.

'I ask you for the last time Jenni, why were you outside!' with each syllable Maxim slammed his fist on the table, then he stood up. This could be it she thought, she might not even get to deliver her half-baked excuse. Jenni could sense that Carl was holding himself back, his body was tense, but he kept silent. Jenni cleared her throat and stared up at the mad Russian, ready to take her chances. It was then that the walky-talky crackled into life. Maxim almost threw his gun across the room but stopped himself. He scrabbled around under some old newspapers and quickly located the walky-talky. Lars' voice was surprisingly clear,

'Gregor, come in it's Thor. Gregor do you read me!! It's an emergency.'

'Ten-four Thor. Go ahead.'

Carl and Jenni did not dare to look at each other. The name Thor was a work of genius as a handle for Lars and his Scandinavian roots and as for Gregor...but before they could enjoy the moment, Thor continued.

'Gregor - it's Brian, I cannot rouse him.'

'What! Is he breathing? over.'

'He is, but I cannot wake him!'

'Stay put Thor. We are coming right away.' Maxim tucked his gun down the waistband of his trousers and turned towards them.

'We all go. Jenni get a jug of cold water, Carl bring the First Aid Kit from the car.' He threw Carl the keys. 'Move!'

Ten minutes later they were all in the outhouse. The cold water had not been a success and the First Aid kit was all but useless.

'Jenni you will try to wake him, I do not want to damage his face by whacking him too hard but...' Jenni didn't need to be asked twice. She knelt beside Brian who was carelessly covered with an old sleeping bag. His face was very pale and she could see the dark circles under his eyes. Jenni swept the strands of his fringe across to one side and gently stroked his cheek.

'I did not ask you to make love to him! Just wake him!'

'Give her a moment Maxim! He may respond to a female voice and come around. Surely it's worth giving it five more minutes?' Carl said, whilst simultaneously giving Jenni the nod to continue.

'OK, but make it quick!'

Brian's pale face felt cool to the touch, but his skin was clammy. A bad sign. Jenni gently turned his head to one side but there was no reaction.

'Brian, can you hear me? It's time to wake up now.'

'Louder!!' Maxim shouted, his patience being overridden by panic. Jenni raised her voice and tried again. No response. Carl then intervened, moving the moth-eaten sleeping bag, and laid a hand on Brian's chest, next he took his pulse.

Finally, he checked his fingernails and Jenni noticed they were discoloured.

'What the fuck have you been giving him!' Carl rarely shouted, but he was angry. 'You can smack him around as much as you want Maxim, he won't come to without urgent treatment. Do something! And now!'

'We could pump his stomach, I'm sure there is some old tubing lying around...'

'He's beyond that point, Lars.' Carl said as he stood up and squared up to Maxim. 'He needs intravenous medication and he needs it now! You must phone the number that Crytex gave you for medical emergencies. I know you have it. If you don't, I will call an ambulance! I will be no party to murder. My brief was to negotiate and protect! Not to kill!'

'This will be seen as a failure. You understand that?' Maxim smashed his closed fist against the rugged brick wall. It must have hurt.

'Lars, fetch the contact book from the car and hurry.'

Maxim made the call. The nearest Crytex medical contact to their location arrived on site within twenty minutes. Lars met the car at the gate and instructed the doctor to park at the side of the cottage. No names were given and few details were exchanged. The doctor, if indeed she was a doctor, examined Brian quickly. She muttered something to herself. Jenni just managed to catch the words, incompetent imbeciles.

'I need a stand, for the drip and some clean bedding. If you could hurry, I'm between appointments.'

Maxim waived his hand towards Lars who scampered off to the cottage.

'Fetch some bedding Jenni. Carl help me to move Brian while we remove the under-sheet.

'What did you give the poor soul?' Maxim handed the doctor the bottle of pills.

'We had to give him more and more.'

'Well of course you did you idiot! His tolerance to the drugs would just increase, surely you know that? What a group of amateurs!'

'It was just meant to be a short-term solution.' Maxim said quietly.

'Well let's hope there are no long-term effects for all your sakes.' The doctor pulled out a large hypodermic needle from her bag. This was Jenni's cue to remove herself from the scene. Needles and drips were not her strong point.

Jenni was allowed to leave the outhouse to locate the clean bedding, she also found a clean T-shirt and tracksuit bottoms in the airing cupboard. Jenni caught up with Lars who was dragging an old hat and coat stand towards the outhouse. After entering, Jenni made up the bed whilst Carl used wet wipes to clean Brian, before dressing him.

'I have given him a Naloxone injection which should reverse the effects of the raised levels of medication that you have been giving him.' She then inserted a cannula in Brian's arm, and connected the drip, hanging the bag of fluid on the hat stand. 'This is saline, to stop him from dehydrating and stabilise his body fluids. You...' the doctor pointed at Jenni. 'After three hours wash your hands, check the level, and replace the bag if it is empty. I will leave five bags of saline. You look a little pale yourself, not a lover of needles then?' This was a rhetorical question. She turned and pointed to Carl. 'And you, in four hours, if the patient has not regained consciousness, give him this.' The doctor showed Carl a pre-filled syringe. Just repeat exactly what you saw me do.' Carl nodded. 'But I say again if he comes around do NOT give him the injection and dispose of this needle with great care. By morning you will have your answer, this will be a long night.' The doctor packed her medical bag and then turned to Maxim, 'Find another way to control him, no more drugs.'

She nodded at Jenni and Carl before leaving the outhouse.

Help me make it through the night

Sammi Smith

Come and lay down by my side
Til the early mornin' light
All I'm takin' is your time
Help me make it through the night

28

Chapter

At the Leonardo Hotel, the pressure was starting to get to us. The late-night knock on the door was not unexpected. At least we three women were bunking up together, poor Andy had lost both of his team-mates and his room must feel very empty.

'Shall I let the Welshy in?' Shauna asked smiling, as she looked across at Berni who was now sporting a rather cosy Marks and Spencer s floral nightie.

'I'm past caring Shauna truth be known.'

'Fine with me.' I added, draping my pale blue towelling dressing gown over my shoulders. Shauna wrenched open the door, bubbling with life as always. She was dressed in a short pink nighty with a cheeky lace edging. Never one for the boring.

Andy paused for a split second, clearly a little taken aback at Shauna's scanty nightwear. There was not much to it.

'Get in here Andy, hope you're bringing gifts.'

'Charming, but now that you mention it.' Andy checked up and down the corridor before entering the room and softly closing the door behind him.

'They are everywhere and just sometimes we need a bit of distance.'

1 4 5

Andy was wearing a Noel Coward-style maroon dressing gown edged with a distinctive blue trim. He sat on the edge of Berni's bed before reaching into one of the inner pockets and pulling out a bottle of vodka.

'Don't ask me how I got this, but the Cloud Nine bar were very accommodating.' The mood lifted, as Berni located miniature mixers from the mini-bar.

'And no we don't give two bleedin' hoots about the extortionate cost of the mini bar, this is on MI5.' Shauna said as she lined the mixer bottles up on the bedside cabinet.

'And bloody Experenta. It's the least they can do.' I swished out the toothbrush glasses from the bathroom. Andy had thoughtfully brought two glasses from his room. He laid out the four glasses and then looked anxiously across at Shauna. Before pouring, Andy knew he had to ask,

'Can you? I mean are you aloud to, you know with the ...'

'Jesus Andy. You can ask me anything. But to save your obvious unease, I will just put it out there. Yes, I am an addict. Yes, I'm always in recovery and yes I am now able to have a drink in controlled situations but never alone. Now if you had a bag of smack or some blow, well that would be very different. One drink then take the bottle away with you. Alcohol I can control, the other shit I can't be near ever again.'

Andy nodded, smiling weakly.

'Don't ask me If I'm fuckin' sure. Just pour the drinks and I'll have lemonade with mine Ta.' Soon everyone had a drink in their hand and we all raised our glasses to toast our lost hero.

'To Brian, wherever you are, we think of you always and with God's speed you'll be back with us soon.'

'Amen.' said Berni quietly.

'Cheers.' I added whilst we clinked glasses.

'Salud!' Shauna shouted before draining her glass and raising it in anticipation.

Andy gently took the glass from her and discreetly pocketed the vodka bottle. The trick was to change tack and take the focus off the alcohol.

'Berni, could I ask if you can sense any news of Brian?'

Berni carefully laid down her half-empty glass of vodka and coke.

'There isn't much peace and quiet or space to reach out to Brian in the chaotic days we've been having. Perhaps I could take a moment now?' She glanced over at Shauna who was already attached to a set of headphones and tapped her foot to the music, whilst giving a wry smile.

'Could we all hold hands and just focus on visualising Brian.' Everyone obeyed including Shauna, who now removed one ear from the headphones. Andy glared at her.

'What? It helps me concentrate and Berni doesn't mind, do you Berni?' Berni shook her head gently, her eyes already closed.

'The picture isn't clear, but I can feel Brian's distress. He's fuzzy-headed. He knows he's trapped and is also restrained in some way. But he is alive and he is fighting. I only hope that he can feel this connection, feel our group pulling together and trying our best to rescue him.'

'Did we get through Berni? I mean sorry to break the spell and all. But are we trying to rescue him or just following soddin' orders from Brown and MI5?'

'Shauna you're on thin ice, I suggest you keep your trap shut.' Andy said, clearly annoyed.

'It's alright.' Berni said quietly, 'I feel sure we got through and Brian knows we are with him.'

'But we're not though are we Berni? We're not fuckin' with him…'

'Shauna that's enough.'

'No she's right we're not physically with him and we have to trust the powers that be to rescue him. But by following the clues and trying our damnedest, Brian will understand that we are doing all we can.'

'So put that in your pipe and smoke it!' Andy said whilst playfully pushing Shauna and ruffling her hair.

'Pillow fight!' she shrieked and grabbed one of the pillows from behind me. She managed to get two swipes in and unsettle Andy before he returned the favour, knocking her off the bed and splitting the pillow. Small pieces of foam spilled across the bedspread and the floor. Pillows were raised for retaliation, which was probably a good time for Brown to arrive. The door swung back, hitting the wall with a loud thud. He was framed beautifully in the doorway, the glare of the bright fluorescent light making his black suit seem even more authoritarian. Shauna and Andy immediately lowered their pillows. I could see Shauna's lip going crooked, a sure sign that she was stifling some inappropriate giggle. Berni glared at her, which was normally sufficient. Sadly not this time. Shauna lowered her head to disguise her smirk and was trying to control her emotions.

The sound that she emitted was the cross between a snort and a sneeze. We all looked at each other for support, but no one could contain themselves. After such a comical sound and the mortified face of Shauna,

I bit my lip, Berni dabbed her mouth with her hanky and Andy pretended he dropped something on the floor.

Brown just stood there, he raised an eyebrow before shaking his head and deftly closing the door. Andy held up his fingers and began counting the seconds until he got to 10. He signalled for us all to hold back until Brown was at least a little further down the corridor. Just as he got to 10, Shauna exploded into hysterical whooping laughter, Andy joined her, Berni laughed a deep throaty laugh and I had one of those belly laughs you normally have when you're at school and someone has broken wind in class. Whether it was the welcome relief from stress or fear or despair, we needed some release and Brian would have joined in wholeheartedly if he'd been here. After things calmed down, we all held hands and said good night to our absent friend, sending our love the only way that we could.

I've Gotta Get a Message to You

Bee Gees

The preacher talked with me and he smiled
Said "Come and walk with me, come and walk one more mile
Now for once in your life you're alone
But you ain't got a dime, there's no time for the phone"
I've just gotta get a message to you
Hold on, hold on
One more hour and my life will be through
Hold on, hold on

29

Chapter

After the doctor left the outhouse, Jenni could tell that Maxim did not take kindly to being told off in such a forthright manner. It was obvious that Brian's health had been impacted by increasing the dose of drugs. Jenni could only hope that Maxim would heed the doctor's warning but knew that being told off by a professional, and a woman to boot, had dented Maxim's ego. They both needed to maintain a low profile. Maxim bristled with irritation and Jenni felt he could explode at any moment. What mattered now was to stabilise Brian and get him through the night. She was praying that Maxim wouldn't want to return to the earlier discussion about her reason for being outside the cottage. She still had no idea who the owner of the drone was and if the arrival of Toby and his sheepdog was just a coincidence. He could have been an agent checking in, it was a good cover, but Maxim was no fool.

'You two, take the first shift.' Maxim pointed towards Jenni and Carl. 'Lars and I need to eat. And don't get any ideas, I do not trust you, either of you. So I am locking you in - no more wandering around and chatting to strange farmers and their dogs when we are meant to be in hiding. The same goes for you Carl, you're soft, like her, not a true Crytex warrior that's for sure.'

'You don't need to lock us in.' Carl said curtly. 'What if we need help or one of us needs the toilet? Maxim sneered, mimicking Carl's words.

'Jesus Christ! This is not a school outing, it is a kidnapping!' Maxim threw the walkie-talkie across to Carl. 'Only use this in an emergency, do you understand?' Jenni and Carl both nodded, anxious for Maxim and his lackey to leave. 'As for the other thing…' Maxim kicked the rusty bucket that Brian had been using, over toward Carl. It stank of stale urine. 'Use this.' Eager to keep the peace and get rid of them, they said nothing. Lars was as excitable as ever, grinning inanely, eager to leave and begin eating and most definitely drinking with his Master.

'If there is any more trouble from either of you, any noise, any stupid messages or tricks then I don't need to tell you what will happen. All three of you are expendable.' Maxim waived his hand dismissively, whilst patting this gun with his other hand. 'The door will be locked until shift change when Lars and I will take over. Brian will either have recovered or no longer be with us.' Maxim shrugged his shoulders somewhat nonchalantly. 'Do what you can, it's in your hands.' Maxim gave Jenni one last piercing glare, before leaving the outhouse and locking the door. They sighed collectively with relief and turned towards each other.

'That was very close. Maxim is one crazy bastard and loony tunes Lars is no better.' Jenni looked down despondently, 'I think my days are numbered.' She waited for Carl to respond, aware that she could be breaking her cover.

Carl looked across at Jenni, he paused and pursed his lips as if to seal the words in his mouth. This was a trust issue for both of them, but for now, they had to keep Brian alive.

'Check the walkie-talkie Carl. Just in case we can get an outside line to Crytex or anyone at all.' Carl grabbed the device and as they suspected it was only connected to Maxim's walky-talky. 'Dammit. Looks like we're stuck in here then.' Jenni looked crestfallen. Carl checked the drips and Jenni realised that at this moment she had to make a judgement call. They were both at risk from the wrath of Maxim and his unpredictability and predilection for violence. Carl had proved himself to be a worthy ally, but should she confide in him? If he was loyal to Crytex and she blew her cover, it would all be over for her. She must tread carefully. But this may be their only chance to speak alone without being overheard or interrupted. Jenni made the decision, she'd start with the drone. But just before she started, Carl moved his stool next to her, and in hushed tones began the conversation.

'I heard it.' he was almost whispering. 'This morning I heard the drone.' Jenni paused, this was the moment that could change things and she knew it.

'Do you think Maxim heard it?'

'I don't know and I don't know who sent it. It wasn't just a random drone that's for sure. Someone was checking up on our location.'

'Is there anything you want to tell me, Carl? This is the time, right now. I know you've always had my back.' Carl paused and then pulled the sheet tightly over Brian.

'This poor devil worries me. How are they going to sedate him now, when they can't drug him any more? Once they get what they want he is expendable. And so are we.'

'I agree with you. But we have each other against those two crazy bastards. How long have you been with Crytex?' Carl paused considering his answer carefully.

'Two years. How about you?' It was Jenni's turn to pause.

'Eighteen months. I know they are dangerous and I have to tell you there is a lot at stake here. The *Watcher 22* program must not get into their hands.' Jenni could hear her heart beating against her rib cage, maybe she had said too much.

'Can I ask you something?' Carl said in almost a whisper. Jenni nodded in response. 'Are you with the British? You know who I mean.'

Jenni knew exactly what Carl meant. This was it. There would be no going back. They could both be killed here anyway. It was time to take a leap of faith. She nodded. No words were needed.

'And you Carl? Are you with the Americans?' There was another long pause. Carl nodded.

'It's time we pulled together Jenni. I need to tell you that I found your stickers, the ones you hid in the handle mattress. You don't need to worry, I disposed of them carefully. If Maxim had found them you would probably be dead by now.'

Carl paused. Jenni just mouthed her thank you and lowered her head. 'Now that we've got that out of the way. I think the drone was ours, it's classic CIA. Toby and the sheepdog smack of your tribe, a typical MI5 job if ever I saw one.' Jenni smiled, Carl was probably right.

'I hope you're not mocking us. Our methods may be a little bit old-fashioned, but they do work. Toby should have established contact and confirmed our location by now. I'm sure he got the measure of Maxim from our conversation.'

'A drone can do all those things, without antagonising Maxim and putting us in danger.'

'That may be the case, but Maxim was inside the cottage when the drone passed over. He couldn't have been identified and neither could we. Toby had positive sightings and interaction which is invaluable in a kidnap situation.' Carl was about to respond, his blue eyes showing just a hint of annoyance when Brian stirred. Carl and Jenni stood up. Jenni checked the drips and Carl moved closer to Brian as if he seemed to be trying to communicate.

'Jenni he's trying to say something. Come over!' Jenni moved to the top of the makeshift bed and put her ear as close to Brian's mouth as she could. He was mumbling, desperately trying to form words with his parched lips.

'Carl get the water! His mouth is too dry.' Carl found a half-empty bottle of water, wiped the top and Jenni lifted Brian's head. Most of it spilled straight back out of Brian's mouth. Jenni wiped his sore lips gently and Brian nodded signalling he wanted more. It was a painstaking process, but finally, Brian shook his head and pursed his lips together. Jenni gently lay his head back on the moth-eaten cushion.

'Can you speak now Brian?' Brian tried to clear his throat. 'Take your time mate you're safe for now and we're all friends here.' Brian shook his head. His eyes began to close and he drifted back off to sleep. 'He's too weak Jenni. Leave him be.' Jenni pulled her fingers through her sleek black hair, a sign that she was under duress.

'I hope you're right Carl, I don't fancy his chances if he tries to communicate when the two idiots are here. Lars might pull Brian's drip out on purpose. He is the more dangerous of the two. We need to use this window of time for planning Carl. It may be our only shot at getting the three of us out of here alive.'

Something inside so strong

Labi Siffre

The higher you build your barriers
The taller I become
The further you take my rights away
The faster I will run

30

Chapter

Shauna's phone alarm was extremely loud. It had been a while since I'd heard *Wake Me Up Before You Go-Go* by Wham! Still, it did the trick and successfully woke us all at 7 am. This was a surprisingly good organisation for Shauna and gave us all the chance to shower and dress and be on time for Brown. This was an important gesture after last night's frivolity. Andy soon joined us in the meeting space and grabbed an orange juice and a croissant as Brown entered the room and signalled for Cagney and Lacey to join us at the table.

'As things are hotting up, and we also know from our source, that Brian's situation is becoming untenable...' Brown paused and glared at Shauna. 'I can say no more and before you ask, the Intel is classified to protect our source.' Shauna thumped her coffee mug down hard on the glass table, this was the signifier of an impending sulk. 'We need to focus on the task at hand. The bank will be opening early to admit Helena and Andy. If the code we receive is easy to decipher and the instructions are clear enough to follow, then we will drive directly to the new location and Cagney will bring Shauna and Berni to meet us there. Now let's move and hopefully get ahead of the game.'

Andy and I were quickly escorted to the car, only having a moment to breathe in some fresh air and get a fleeting glance of the City as it awoke. There was little traffic and soon enough Lacey was opening the heavy door of the Range Rover and escorting us back toward the bank. Freddie immediately let us in and followed the well-practised protocol. It was beginning to feel a little bit like Groundhog Day.

I sat in my usual seat. And again Andy returned quickly and winked confidently at me on his return, indicating his head toward the exit. It all worked seamlessly, we left by the back exit and the Range Rover was waiting. Brown looked flustered and unusually unprepared.

'The message is as weird as ever.' Andy said whilst shaking his head. 'Do we have a secure phone line, Brown?'

'Lacey, pass me the burner, the one for emergencies. Explain yourself, Andy.'

'It's just a name on a piece of paper 'Archie' no surname and a phone number. The other sentence means nothing to me, it says 'Tell Archie it's time' and then there's a password, in Latin, and five crossword type clues.'

'Make the call Andy. There's no point in moving until we know what the hell is going on.'

'I disagree Brown. It's too obvious waiting here. Let me drive and get some distance between us and the bank.'

'Very well Lacey, you drive. Andy, you make the call.'

Andy punched in the number and waited. There was no response. It was quite early after all. He tried again, but nothing, and there was no answering machine. But the third time proved to be lucky.

'Who the hell is this? Calling at this hour.'

Andy took a deep breath, 'Archie it's time.'

Silence. Nothing.

'Say again.'

'Archie it's time.'

'Jesus. I was wondering when your lot would show up. Is Brown with you?'

'He is.'

'Put him on.' Andy handed the phone to Brown.

'Brown?'

'It is indeed.'

'Tell me which team you support and their home ground.' Brown hesitated and a slight flush came to his cheeks.

'As Barry well knew, I despise football, I'm a cricket man, Lancashire cricket club to be precise. And it's Old Trafford Cricket Ground.'

'Stop there. He said you'd say that and start banging on. Andy, are you there mate?'

'I am.'

'Assuming Helena's there too?'

'She is.'

'I'll meet you opposite the Royal Exchange Theatre in twenty minutes. You'll know me by my grey fedora hat and tweed overcoat. You should have the password.' and with that, the line went dead.

'Lacey get us there. I think we might need the whole team together. I'll contact Cagney.'

Within a quarter of an hour, everyone was there and discreetly positioned along St Ann's Square. Brown and Andy were the closest to the entrance. Shauna was window shopping with Lacey. Cagney was stationed directly opposite the entrance of the theatre, checking for any unexpected visitors. Berni and I walked a circuit, close enough to be summoned if needed. Archie was true to his word and dressed as described. Cagney alerted us to his arrival and each couple completed a measured approach to the entrance. Berni and I got there just in time to witness the somewhat awkward shaking of hands and I could just hear Andy whisper the words, 'impetro lost'.

'Berni you know Latin, what does that mean?' I asked. Berni gave a little giggle.

'It means get lost.'

Archie nodded his head and smiled.

'Good old Barry!' he said whilst shaking Andy's hand. 'No one else would have that as a password.'

'Let me introduce myself. I'm Archie one of the Trustees on the Board of this magnificent theatre.' He pulled out an impressive set of keys, ran up the set of steps to the left of the main entrance, unlocked the door, and entered a code into the alarm, before signalling us all to follow him inside. He held the door open and told us to mount the next set of stairs, before carefully locking the door and resetting the code. It was like entering a different world. Your eyes are drawn to the columns and high ceiling and beautiful glazed domes. Archie bubbled with excitement and enthusiasm.

'Let me tell you a potted history. This colossal space was one of the world's centres for cotton trade until the Second World War. Then the building took a direct hit during the Manchester blitz. It was threatened with demolition and lay unused and empty until a theatre company took up residence in 1973. This is now the largest 'in-the-round' theatre space in the country.

A theatre space in which the audience surrounds the acting area.'

We were all bowled over by the sheer splendour of the Royal Exchange Theatre and its airy space and beautiful design. Archie walked us further into the building, clearly proud of this amazing theatre. The seven-sided theatre module is a feat of engineering and weighs in at 150 tonnes, suspended from four of the Hall's enormous columns,

'The second and third floors have Corinthian columns and ...' As usual it was Brown who broke the spell, he had only one agenda.

'Sorry to interrupt Archie, it is breathtaking...'

'But you're here for a reason.' Archie said and brushed the brim of his fedora in recognition. 'All I know is that I have to ask you to cast your gaze on that.' He pointed toward one of the domes. 'Look just below the dome, that's the original trading board with the day's closing figures.' There were three black information boards, side by side but set high up, just below the dome. 'That's your connection, for the code, that's all I know.'

I could hear the faint sound of music in the distance and I'm sure there was a chuckle.

Drop the Pilot

Joan Armatrading

I'm right on target, my aim is straight
So you're in love, I say what of it?
Things can change, there's always changes
I wanna try some rearranging, I say
Drop the pilot, try my balloon

31

Chapter

Brian was still sleeping. His colour gradually began to improve, the drips were helping to stabilise him. Jenni felt a huge sense of relief now that she knew her American ally, Carl, was on board. Two agencies were now involved instead of one and she no longer felt as isolated and vulnerable. Now was the time to exchange notes and plan their next move. Maxim had unwittingly done them both a favour by locking them in the outhouse together. It was rare that they got uninterrupted time alone. For now, at least, they were away from the mad pair and could look after Brian and help him to recover.

'What was your brief Jenni? Why were you sent here?' Carl asked gently. Jenni moved across to the door and rattled it, pulling down hard on the handle but it was locked and there was no forcing it. She found a crack that she could peer through and checked that Maxim and Lars were not on their way back. For now, at least they had some unsupervised time to talk. Jenni walked over to Brian's bedside, and they seized the opportunity to share information.

'MI5 have had Maxim under surveillance for some time. I was enlisted in the Crytex training programme to

161

infiltrate his team and gather information. Our focus was to prevent *Watcher 22* from falling into their hands following Barry's suspicious death. That's it in a nutshell. And yourself?'

'After working in the field for the 'Americans', my next assignment was to infiltrate Crytex. They are no fools, it took me two attempts to be accepted as a negotiator and three more missions before I became involved in this madness. My role was to ensure that Maxim didn't overstep the boundaries and like you, I was instructed to stop Crytex from procuring *Watcher 22*. So here we are, both with similar goals, but now our priority is to save Brian's life and escape with whatever information we can. If we can get Brian out it will reduce the leverage Crytex has over the team. Up to now our contact with Brian has been restricted, this is our chance and it may be our only chance.'

'I agree Carl. But even if Brian does wake up and we can get him up and mobile, we will need support. Do you have CIA operatives nearby? I know Toby has a farm over the hill, but I don't think Brian will be able to walk there. Do you have a messaging system, a way of attracting them for an intervention?'

'They searched me and took my phone. We're going to have to get the car keys. It's the only way we will get out of here alive.'

'I haven't managed to get any Intel on Crytex though Carl, I've been too busy protecting my cover and myself. But if we manage to escape with Brian, then at least the hold they have on the team will be removed. We will have to overpower them to get the car and get Brian out. What if the drone was from Crytex and they are watching the cottage?'

'Then we have to get to Toby and pray he's one of yours. If he is, there will be a plan in place to get us away.'

'And if he isn't?'

'Then we'll just take his car and leave him be.'

'I guess that's all we can do. We will need to ditch the Land Rover as soon as we can. Crytex will be able to track it.'

'If Toby is one of yours, then he can take it for a spin.' Jenni nodded in agreement.

'I think we might be getting a bit ahead of ourselves though. We have to get out of here first.'

'We need to catch them off guard and we'll need a weapon, something to threaten them with. Maxim is armed and also the holder of the only car key. We can't jump-start the Range Rover, I'm just praying it's not fingertip recognition.'

'It's not. I watched Maxim use the key. But you're right we can't start the car without his key.'

'We need an old farm tool or a spade, something we can jump them with.'

Neither of them had taken much notice of their surroundings until now, their main priority had been to take care of Brian. The outhouse was made of stone, with a slated roof and a thick wooden door. The only light was from a portable LED camping lamp which was battery-powered and hung on a hook by Brian's bed. Carl unhooked it and began searching the outhouse. Brian muttered to himself and tried to turn over. Jenni calmed him. Brian needed to stay on his back as he had a drip in each arm. Meanwhile, Carl had found a pile of rotting wood in one of the corners and was secretly praying for an axe to magically appear. No such luck. He placed the lantern down on the ground and began moving the rotten timber. There was nothing there that could help them. He sighed and then carefully stacked the rotting wood back against the wall. But then, just as Jenni turned to speak to Carl, she noticed something on the ground. It must have been disturbed when Carl had moved the wood.

'Carl stand back !' Jenni said excitedly. 'Turn to the right. Move the lantern close to your right foot. I see something, a long thin oblong shape.' Carl turned and brought the light down to floor level.

'I don't see it Jenni.' Jenni walked across slowly keeping her eyes fixed on the object. The light in the small outhouse was poor and her vision was not good in the half-light. She knelt down and brushed the hay to one side before grabbing the rusty file. It was about six inches in length and although it was very dirty, it was solid and the double-cut teeth were still evident.

'Jenni that's a great find! Just brilliant.' Carl reached out his hand to have a hold of the rusty file. 'It's perfect, I can feel myself holding this against Maxim's throat right now.' he said, with an air of longing. 'Let's hide it under Brian's blankets.' The pair moved back across to the makeshift bed and Carl tucked it safely under the thin straw mattress. 'We need something else. Jenni, you go and look whilst I change Brian's drip.' Jenni moved to the opposite corner, but there were no more surprises. She crouched down and used the lantern to methodically scan the floor, moving the hay with her hands. It didn't take long to sweep the room.

'It won't be enough Carl. We both need to have a weapon of some sort if we are going to stand a chance.'

Carl sighed, he dutifully attached the drips, before patting Brian's hand and taking a seat beside her.

'You're right Jenni. But that's all we have.' The walky-talky interrupted Carl as it crackled into life. Jenni flinched, she needed the two idiots to keep out of the way for a bit longer, while they got organised and Brian's condition improved. It was Maxim's voice that greeted them.

'Come in Bonnie and Clyde, Gregor wants an update. Over.'

Carl picked up the walkie-talkie and dutifully used Maxim's absurd nickname for him.

'Clyde here. Over. The patient is still asleep, but he is improving. Over.'

'Good. Thor and I will be with you in an hour, to check on you. What's that Thor? No, not yet. Thor wants to play the hunting game. But for now, you both are useful to me. Over and out.'

'God only knows what the hunting game involves, but I think we would be the prey.' Jenni said quietly. Carl was careful to switch off the walkie-talkie.

'We have less time than I thought. How do you want to play this Jenni?'

'We will have to get Brian over in that corner and prop him up using the wood.'

'Then make the bed look as though he is still in it.'

'Agreed. Now we have to decide who has the file. Perhaps...' Carl was interrupted by Brian, who was making grunting noises.

'Jenni move closer to him and see if you can make out what he's saying.' Jenni leaned forward to Brian and could just make out a few words.

'I think he can hear what we're saying. He keeps saying bed and pushing the mattress down with his elbow.'

'Let's roll him and see if there's something else under the mattress.' They carefully rolled Brian over and Carl held him on his side whilst Jenni lifted the mattress. What can you see Jenni?'

'There's the rusty file and just some wooden slats. Carl, we can use them to knock one of the idiots out. We have our two weapons. Thank you Brian. It's game on!'

Eye of the tiger

Survivor

It's the eye of the tiger
It's the thrill of the fight
Rising up to the challenge of our rival

32

Chapter

I didn't understand the subtleties of Flint's song choice, *Drop the Pilot,* until we were all positioned opposite the trading board. Andy was searching his pockets for the sheet of notes he had collected from the bank. Shauna was shuffling impatiently as usual and Berni was still in awe of the magnificent theatre. That's when I realised the connection between the song and the theatre and gave out a mini snort.

'Jesus Helena. What was that about?'

'Joan Armatrading, Flint's song, very clever, the trading is the link.'

'Berni, Helena's gone fuckin' nuts.' Shauna said while doing the circular symbol around the side of her head. I occasionally forgot that not everyone hears the music.

'OK ladies, let's focus. I have it here.'

'At last! We're wasting time, time that we should be spending on rescuing Brian, especially when some bastard knows where he is or has an 'undercover contact.' Shauna shot an accusatory glance over at Brown. I looked over at Andy willing him to get on with it. I took Shauna's arm to reassure her.

'Let's just listen to the clue Shauna. That's how we help Brian.' Andy cleared his throat for effect.

'There are just these five crossword-type clues.'

Berni had already organised pen and paper. Brown just looked agitated and Lacey kept a close eye on the door, keeping in contact with Cagney who was outside. No one was taking any chances, the closer we got the more dangerous it got.

'Right now listen up, this is what the first clue says. Second board, centre - New Year's Eve, date.' Everyone looked around and seconds later there was a familiar shriek from Shauna.

'It's the bloody trading board!' Shauna pointed toward it excitedly. I knew that Flint had been right, but kept it to myself. Andy patted Shauna on the back, Brown nodded and I squeezed her arm.

'Well done Shauna, very good.' Berni said as she walked over to the Trading Board.

'Ooh let me be the pointer, I bloody love things like this!' Archie located a long pole and passed it to her, it had probably been used to open high windows in the past. Obviously, it didn't reach, but it would do as a guide and it kept Shauna happy.

'Read the clue again Andy, let's do it right from the start.' With a half smile, Andy read the clue again. Shauna was taking her new-found role very seriously and dutifully pointed towards the very top of the board, which displayed the last day of trading.

'Remember to read it very carefully. Barry could be quite particular.' Brown said solemnly.

'Ah, I get it. It's not the month of the year it's the actual date, he's after. It's 31. Jot that down Berni. It's number 31.'

Berni duly noted the number as Shauna asked excitedly for the next clue.

'Third board - 'Friends' can be found here.' I knew the answer before even looking at the board, but there was no way any of us would spoil Shauna's fun. But just before the pointer landed on it, I could resist no longer.

'New York!'

'Bloody hell that was fast H.'

'The clue was in the reference to 'Friends', but good to have it clarified officially by the board.'

'Helena's right, there's no room for guessing when a man's life is at stake.' Brown knew how to dampen the party spirit. Berni intervened before Shauna had time to respond.

'Clue 3 Andy if you please.'

'Third board, 5 Down,' Andy paused while Shauna counted the spaces. 'What's the first word?'

'Exchange. 'Shauna said excitedly. 'Now we need the second and fifth letters, letters 2 and 5. That's X and A!'

'Great stuff it makes no sense, but well done. Berni, what do we have so far?'

'We have 31, New York, XA. Does that mean anything to anyone?' I took a sneaky glance over at Brown and noticed that he was looking shifty.

'Brown do you know something, you have that 'look'.' Brown was no lover of the spotlight and waived his hand dismissively.

'Is there one final clue? If so I need to hear it.' Brown said somewhat brusquely.

'Here it is then.' Andy said, picking up on Brown's mood. 'First Board, first-word abbreviate.' Shauna shouted the word before anyone else had seen it.

'Alexandria! How does that fuckin' help?'

'It's Alex, but Brown how does that help?' I asked, looking directly at him.

Brown beckoned us all away from the board, Shauna replaced the pointer pole and we all sat at one of the cafe tables.

'Read it back one more time please Berni.'

'31, New York, XA, Alex.'

Brown paused. 'Lacey check this on the secure site, I will reorder the clue.'

Lacey pulled out a small tablet, which immediately came on, MI5 technology was the best.

'XA31, New York, Alex Mallory.'

Within seconds Lacey nodded his head. 'It's as you thought Brown and...'

'Jesus what the fuckin....' It was time to close Shauna down. This was very serious.

'Brown, it's time to explain.'

'It's complicated. Barry has done his research, he was such a clever man.'

'Barry was a clever man. Meanwhile, Brian fights for his life and we don't know what the hell is going on. So if you could just explain! This fuckin' game has gone far enough...'

'That's enough Shauna.' Berni said firmly. 'Over to you Brown and we don't need the complicated version, we have all worked hard to get to this point.' We all looked across at Brown and our collective stare did the trick.

'Very well. Archie if you could give us five minutes.' Brown paused and Archie walked away, looking relieved 'The potted version is this. Put simply XA31 was developed by Alex Mallory. A refined version of XA21.' I could feel Shauna's heckles rising and I gave Brown the symbol for moving things on.

'There was a blackout triggered by a local outage and it went undetected due to a problem with the XA21 monitoring software.' Shauna was now tapping her foot, a clear sign she was ready to blow. Andy jumped in.

'And this is relevant because?'

'It's relevant because the bug was discovered by Alex Mallory during an intensive code audit and it took weeks of pouring through millions of lines of code and data to find it. The blackout occurred at a time when the Blaster computer worm was wreaking havoc across the Internet. The timing triggered some speculation that the virus may have played a role in the outage. In simple terms, if you want to stop *Watcher 22* and remove it from the world then this could be the way. XA31 is probably a more refined version of XA21 and could be the solution to our problem.'

'No wonder the kidnappers want to stop us, if they get to know about this, things will escalate.' Andy said quietly.

'Cagney, inform MI6. Lacey, get us back to the hotel. We need to move and quickly. Oh and did I mention we are going to a different hotel, all your belongings have been moved. Another data breach I'm afraid.'

I can see clearly

Johnny Nash

I can see clearly now, the rain is gone,
I can see all obstacles in my way
Gone are the dark clouds that had me blind
It's gonna be a bright (bright), bright (bright)
Sun-Shiny day.

33

Chapter

As luck would have it Carl still had his fancy military watch, despite the trouble it had almost got him into. At least they had some idea of the time scale now, even though Maxim could never be relied upon with his timings. Maxim had said that he and Lars would return in an hour, but that could mean anything.

'Right Jenni, there's no time to waste. Those idiots could arrive at any time.'

'I agree. I think it might be better if you take the piece of wood from the bed and whack Maxim with it, you can put more power behind it, Carl. He needs taking out first. I'll go for Lars, hopefully a rusty file being held to his throat will be enough to control him. You get the keys from Maxim and if he doesn't have the car key, at least we can lock them both in the outhouse and have time to search for the keys inside the house.'

'Good thinking Jenni. Once they are locked in the outhouse we can focus on our next step.' Jenni nodded in agreement. 'We need to move Brian now, just to keep him safe if it all kicks off. Also if Maxim is out for the count, we can tie Lars to the bed.' Carl nodded his agreement as he unhooked Brian's drips from the makeshift stand and gently tucked the bags of fluid inside his shirt. He still needed them, of that there was no doubt. Jenni moved across to the left-hand corner of the outhouse and rearranged the rotting pieces of wood, making Brian a makeshift seat. This meant that he would be hidden from view, as the door opened from right to left. Carl explained the plan to Brian as they walked him gently to the makeshift seat. Brian lowered himself down and Jenni carefully leaned Brian's head against the brick wall.

'There you go Brian. Do you feel secure? We don't want you falling to the ground and alerting those idiots to our plan.' Brian nodded. His lips set in a determined line. He was managing to keep his eyes half open, he knew what was at stake.

Carl and Jenni pulled the old sheet off the mattress and made it into the shape of a body. They stuffed it under the threadbare blanket and then both stood back to assess their handiwork. Without intense inspection, it did look as though a body was in the bed.

'We need to move the light away from the bed, then it won't be as noticeable.'

They moved the light to the back left-hand corner which worked well.

'Let's not forget that we have the advantage of surprise, but we do need to think carefully about where we position ourselves. Once the door is opened, the light will flood in. I think I should stand behind the door ready to whack Maxim.' Carl said, squinting his eyes as he tried to visualise the scenario. 'We'll have to try and get him to walk as far into the room as possible. Once he's down Lars will panic and hopefully run over to his Master. That's when you slam the door Jenni, to stop him running away. You must get the file to his throat. If all goes to plan we can get the keys and the car and make our escape.'

'It's a lot to do Carl, things can happen very quickly. If Lars manages to escape, he will raise the alarm in whatever way he can. We must secure them both in the outhouse if we're going to stand a chance.'

'I agree Jenni. We mustn't falter.' Carl took a deep breath and just for a moment there was silence.

Jenni looked across at Brian, he was slumped in an awkward position but remained upright. He made a grunting noise, the same noise as when he alerted them to the wooden bed slats. Jenni went across to him as he raised his arm which took a lot of effort. He was pointing to the medication which had been carelessly left by Brian's bed. Carl walked across the room and examined the discarded bottles. Brian became more excited and managed to utter two words. 'Drug them.'

'Great idea mate. I'll check the bottles now.' Carl shook each one of the white plastic pill bottles, of which there were many. There were plenty of bottles as Maxim had planned to drug Brian indefinitely. Jenni pitched in to help and began putting the empty containers in a pile. It made her realise just how many tablets Brian had been forced to take. In minutes Carl found a new bottle that had not been opened. He checked that the label was the same as the others, the last thing they needed was to pump their prisoners full of Speed. Jenni confirmed that it was the same sleeping drug that had been given to Brian and they knew how powerful that was. 'Good thinking Brian! They deserve a taste of their own medicine.' Carl checked his watch. Half an hour had passed. 'We need to get into position now.' Carl picked up his wooden bed slat and stood behind the door, next to where Brian was sitting. Jenni grabbed the rusty file and perched on the edge of Brian's bed which was a couple of feet from the door. Carl checked his watch again and then grabbed the piece of wood with two hands ready to swing it at Maxim's head. Jenni tucked the rusty file under her thigh. They were ready and waiting. This was their chance to not only save Brian but to also save themselves.

It was a good job they were ready. Maxim and Lars arrived early. They heard the sound of the key turning in the lock and gave each other nods of reassurance. Maxim sauntered in first, he glared at Jenni and Lars scampered in behind him.

'Where's Carl?' he asked as Lars hopped impatiently from foot to foot. He got his answer as Carl pushed back the door and then whacked Maxim across his head with such force that he fell to the ground. Lars panicked and ran over to his Master and as he turned Jenni sprang up from the bed and pushed the rusty file against his neck.

'Sit on the bed Lars, now!' Jenni said in a measured tone and jabbed the file a little further into his neck to show that she meant business. Carl checked on Maxim, he was out cold, and a trickle of blood oozed from the back of his head. So far so good. Jenni reached for the bottle of sleeping tablets and gave them to Carl. He unscrewed the lid and took out a handful.

'Your turn to be drugged, Lars.' Carl grabbed his feet and swung them up onto the bed. 'Tip back your head, open your mouth!' Carl pushed the tablets into Lars' mouth and grabbed the half-empty water bottle and forced Lars to swallow. After checking his mouth was clear of tablets, he made Lars lie down.

'Look at this Carl, what a gift.' Jenni said as she pointed to a rope that Lars had attached to his belt. 'Was this for the hunting game Lars?' Lars nodded, clearly in a state of shock.

'We'll be having that.' Carl said pulling the rope off Lars' belt. 'Let's tie you to the bed first and then we can use the rest of the rope to tie Maxim's hands. So glad you have your hunting knife with you Lars. Just perfect, you thought of everything.'

Once Lars was secured. Carl checked Maxim's pockets. Luck was with them and the car key was on the same keyring as the outhouse key. Carl tied Maxim's hands and signalled for Jenni to help roll him under the bed. Mission accomplished. Lars could barely keep his eyes open and had stopped wriggling now. This was it! Carl checked the knots were secure and Jenni grabbed both walkie-talkies and made sure Carl had theirs.

'Now we can move Brian.' They helped Brian to his feet and walked him slowly out of the door, propping him up against the wall. Brian shielded his eyes with his hand as the light hurt his eyes, but he welcomed it. There was a collective sigh of relief as Carl locked the outhouse door. Stage one had been completed. But just when they felt they could take a breather, that they could take stock and regroup, there was a familiar noise overhead. It was the drone, it was back and they were out in the open.

Don't Stop Believin'

Journey

Don't stop believin'
Hold on to that feelin'
Streetlights, people
Don't stop believin'

34

Chapter

There was no time to lose and so much at stake. The drone was circling the farm and each time it circled, it got lower and lower. Carl unlocked the car, and they manoeuvred Brian into an upright position.

'Can it fire on us? The drone, is it armed?' Jenni asked as Carl started the engine and hurriedly put on his seat belt.

'The drone's too small to be armed, it's not military grade. But what we don't know is how close the Crytex agents are and when they'll be here.' The tyres screeched as Carl quickly reversed out onto the small country lane.

'Jesus Carl! Don't get us killed before we start!' She was very aware that Brian was unsecured on the back seat. They approached a small junction. The drone was still in pursuit.

'Which way Jenni?' Carl asked as he came to a sudden stop.

'I don't know. Toby just pointed over to the right, all he said was that his farm was over the next hill.'

'I'll take the right turn then. You do realise that Toby could just be a regular farmer?'

'It's a risk we'll have to take.' Jenni paused before adding, 'I don't believe in coincidences and it's not as if we have anywhere else to go out here in the sticks.' Carl drove at high speed along the narrow country lanes. Jenni was desperately trying to catch sight of the drone. Meanwhile, Brian, who had been rolling around on the back seat of the Range Rover, managed to secure the middle seat belt around his waist. The thought of being hurled through the front window was incentive enough. This was not his time to die, he decided. He was becoming more alert and any sense of discomfort was easily outweighed by the joy of escape not only from the drugs but also from his captors. As his usefulness to Crytex had waned, Brian knew that his days were numbered.

Although Carl and Jenni knew that the drone was following them, it was almost impossible to assess its exact position as the car pitched from side to side. This really did feel like a 'road less travelled.' Suddenly the question about the drone's whereabouts was answered for them as it was heading straight into the windscreen. Jenni had forgotten how violent an emergency stop was. The seat belts locked as they jerked forward, but fortunately, the air-bags did not deploy. After the initial shock wore off, Jenni turned to check on Brian. Thankfully Brian's seat belt had done its job. He had been knocked around a little but nodded confidently when has was asked if he was OK. Jenni took a deep breath and Carl patted her arm and that's when she noticed a small trickle of blood running down from his forehead. He immediately wiped it away and dismissed it.

'It's nothing, I just banged the side of my head. It's an old wound. It often reopens, it's nothing.'

Jenni silently passed Carl a tissue and he wiped the blood away. 'I need to check the car for damage.' he said as he opened the car door.

'It's unbelievable, the drone didn't even dint or shatter the windscreen!' Carl said in amazement. 'It just bounced right off the glass.'

'We've been so lucky.' Jenni said before taking a deep breath. Have you found the drone?'

'Not yet. Can you help me find it Jenni?' Jenni joined Carl in the search and it was soon located, it had veered off the windscreen and landed on the verge of the road under some bushes. Although the windscreen was unscathed by the head-on collision, the drone was a little worse for wear. The black multi-rotor drone lay on its back, making a mechanical whirring sound and the green 'power on' indicator light was flashing on and off. Carl wasted no time in smashing it with a rock, making sure he removed the cameras 'They can track us to this exact location Jenni! The drone may be destroyed but they'll be coming for us. Let's go!' Without further ado, Carl kicked the drone back under the bushes and they got back into the Land Rover. They needed to find Toby's farm and quickly.

Carl wasted no time, he drove as fast as he could. As they went over the brow of the hill, Jenni spotted a farm building in the distance. They hurtled towards it, Jenni directing Carl as best she could. He was doing a sterling job, taking the tight bends at speed and negotiating the many potholes along the rugged farm tracks. Within ten minutes they were approaching the farmhouse and Jenni said a silent prayer that Toby would turn out to be more than just a friendly farmer. She needn't have worried. Toby was obviously in the know. He was waiting at the farm entrance with a military sniper rifle slung over his shoulder, a firearm that no farmer would possess. Carl had been right, he was one of theirs. Carl brought the Land Rover to a sudden stop and Brian gave an involuntary groan.

'Greetings neighbours. It's so good to see you. I was hoping for a visit.' Toby smiled as did Jenni, his modest use of understatement confirmed his MI5 status, to her at least. 'I knew something was up when the drone went up again. Did you take it out?'

'It took itself out, it flew head-on into our windscreen. No damage and we located the drone and smashed it into pieces. But we feel sure that Crytex will be on their way, they have our last location from when the drone crashed and it's not that far from here.'

'We need to move it then.' Toby threw Jenni a bunch of keys. 'You need to switch vehicles. Head to the barn, the door is open.' Toby paused for a moment. 'Sorry, I don't know your name?'

'It's for the best.' Carl snapped. 'Let's just get Brian out of the Land Rover.'

Jenni ran to the barn and jumped into a moonstone grey, 4-door Golf and drove it out onto the forecourt. It had a surprisingly powerful engine and she had to bring it to a sudden stop. Carl turned to glare at Toby.

'Jesus! What the hell?'

'It's had a few modifications, courtesy of you know who.' Toby winked at Jenni. 'I'll take the Land Rover and drive in the opposite direction.'

'Very chummy.' Carl said sarcastically. 'Now if we could get Brian into the car.' Within minutes they had swapped cars and Brian was safely strapped in the back seat of the Golf. This time he was sat upright, on his insistence. Toby had instructed them to bear left and head for the dual carriageway and that's exactly what Jenni did.

'Any comments on my driving and you can walk.' Jenni said firmly.

'I won't say a word.' Carl said turning his head away, disguising a smile.

'Do you think they'll send up another drone?'

'Who knows? But they will come for us, of that I am sure. Rescuing Brian reduces the leverage that Crytex have over the Team and subsequently their chances of acquiring *Watcher 22*. It's imperative that we don't get caught and Brian must not get recaptured. Jenni could hear Brian muttering his ascent from the back seat. Jenni brought the Golf to a sudden halt as they approached a crossroads.

There was no one behind them as yet, but time was ticking.

'Straight on.' Brian said from the back of the car.

'He's right. We can't risk doubling back on ourselves.'

Jenni drove the car straight across and put her foot down. This road was much smoother and in the distance they could see the signs of a busy dual-carriageway.

'Almost there, thank God.' She had spoken too soon. A black Land Rover, the same make as Maxim's, was travelling at speed on the opposite side of the road. It shot past them and then slammed on its brakes.

'It's clocked us. We'll never outrun it. Get on the dual carriageway Jenni! Let's go!'

The Land Rover had to complete a tricky three-point turn as Jenni drove the Golf onto the dual carriageway. They were desperately in need of a plan or some backup or both. Maybe Toby had called it in. Jenni drove the

Golf as fast as she could. Carl was scanning the traffic behind them.

'I see them, they're not that far behind us!'

'Don't let them take me again.' Brian said emotionally. 'I'm a Social Worker, not a spy.' And that's when it happened. Two unmarked police cars with lights and sirens blaring flew down the hard shoulder. One stayed behind the Golf and the other overtook them and positioned directly in front of their car. They had their escort to safety at long last, or had they?

Runaway Baby

Bruno Mars

Run, run, run away, run away, baby
Before I put my spell on you
You better get, get, get away, get away, darling
'Cause everything you heard is true
So you better run, run, run away, run away, baby

When people say that they remember seeing things in slow motion Jenni never really believed them, until now. The relief at being escorted by the unmarked police cars gave them all a sense of new-found confidence. But Crytex would not give up so easily. They had all assumed that the Land Rover behind them would back off, it didn't, despite the police presence. That was how confident and arrogant Crytex had become. Within minutes another Land Rover joined its counterpart behind the police car and began gaining on them. Then came the whirring sound of a much larger drone overhead, the noise became louder as it circled lower and lower. But not for much longer.

No one heard the sound of the shot, but one had been fired. The drone was clipped and knocked off its course before crash landing into a nearby field.

'I think we owe your friend Toby a big thank you for that. I'm betting he fired that sniper rifle from one of the hills we just passed.'

'Great shot.' Jenni said proudly and Brian muttered his agreement from the back seat.

'Let's not forget, that was quite a risk he took. The drone could have landed on the road or on one of the vehicles and caused an accident.' Carl added curtly.

'Well, it didn't. Now we only have the Land Rovers to worry about and not the pesky drone.' Just as Jenni said that, one of the Land Rovers behind them veered onto the hard shoulder, passing the police car and approaching at speed. This time they heard the shot. Carl turned just in time and managed to spot one of the Tactical Firearms Commanders (TFC's) quickly retracting his weapon and pulling his arm back through the left-hand window of the police car. The Land Rover swung off the road and came to an abrupt stop, the back tyre had been shot out.

'Wow! Great shot!' Carl said, clearly impressed.

'Indeed it was, but wasn't that a bit risky on a public highway?'

'You're not complaining are you Jenni? There's still one Land Rover left behind us. It looks like it's backing off.'

Brian gave a muffled cheer and Jenni joined in with a whoop. 'But I don't think they'll give up that easily.' Carl said shaking his head.

'Oh no! Look there's a slip road ahead, on the left. Do you recognise those vehicles? Oh God, not more Land Rovers!' All they could do was watch as the Land Rovers sped down the slip road in front of the convoy of cars and that's when they slammed on their brakes. All six vehicles had to perform an emergency stop.

The sound of screeching tyres could be heard from miles away. The police car behind the Golf had to swerve hard left onto the hard shoulder to avoid a collision. Then, all hell broke loose. One of the Armed Response

Vehicle Officers (ARV officers) from the lead car ran back to the Golf and jumped in the back with Brian.

'Get your heads down! Now!' he dragged Brian across the seat, then opened the window resting his loaded weapon on the sill. Next, the two-way radio crackled into life and he confirmed that their 'asset' was safe. Within seconds of the message being received, the police activity picked up.

'MI5 knows where we are. Stay low, back up is on its way.'

Four people, dressed from top to toe in black with matching balaclavas, got out of the two lead Land Rovers and moved to the front of the vehicles for protection. The two ARV officers from the rear vehicle had a difficult choice to make. Both left the police car together, one remained at the boot of the Golf whilst the other sidled past them to join the policewoman. So far, no shots had been fired. There was only one Crytex operative in the Land Rover at the rear which evened up the odds a little.

'Give me a weapon.' Carl said to one of the ARV officers 'I'm unarmed. We have no protection at all upfront. At least give us a fighting chance if things go wrong. We are trained government agents and we know you've been briefed.' Silence. No words were spoken as the gun was handed over. Carl checked the weapon. Jenni nodded, her mobility was more restricted due to the steering wheel, whereas Carl could just jump out if necessary.

The seriousness of the situation was lost on no one. The Crytex team were hired thugs, military muscle scooped up from the bottom of a very dirty barrel. There would be no limits and no boundaries. Strategically this was a nightmare for the police. They had little information regarding the group's weaponry which posed a significant risk as they could be armed with incendiary devices. The money would be no object for a company like Crytex and its international backers. The ARV officers were well armed with Glock 17 self-loading pistols, shotguns and tasers, but this was a public highway and although the dual carriageway had been closed and cleared, there was always a risk of potential harm to a member of the public. Also, Brian was a civilian, innocently caught up in this very dangerous situation.

Jenni looked across at Carl. 'We're sitting ducks in this car. Brian is protected back there by ARV officers. We know it's Brian they will come for. God only knows what they are capable of.'

'We sit tight for now.' said the policeman. 'That's the orders.'

'I don't think they'll throw a device at the Golf and risk injuring Brian. So we stay put, for now at least.'

Just as Carl finished speaking there was an almighty bang, followed by two more explosions and smoke enveloped the car. The police car in front of them burst into flames and one of the police officers who had been standing to the right of the front car was crawling towards the Golf. Carl didn't hesitate, he opened his door, crouched down low and dragged the police officer to his feet. Brian's policeman opened the car door and between the two of them, they got the injured policeman inside. He was winded by the blasts, but he wasn't seriously injured.

'Go back for Officer Courtney!' the Police Officer said rather breathlessly, 'She was on the left side of the road. I can't get her on my radio. Don't let them take her.' Carl patted his arm, gave Jenni a reassuring nod, and closed the car door.

He withdrew his weapon and took a deep breath. Now he had to choose between going solo or teaming up with the police officer who was situated at the boot of the Golf. He made a split-second decision, they needed that Officer in situ guarding the Golf and Carl was closer to make the rescue. He could only assume that Officer Courtney had been blown outwards by the blast. The smoke was starting to clear and still, there was no movement from the Crytex scum, he needed to act quickly. Carl kept his head very low and ran slowly over to the boot of the police car. He checked behind him before peering around the car and scanning the hard shoulder. There was a camber on the hard shoulder, if Officer Courtney had been blown sideways she may have rolled down into the field.

There was no other choice, Carl rolled himself across the hard shoulder. And that was when he saw her, Officer Courtney. He crawled towards her across the gritty surface. Her eyes were closed and she was covered in blood. Carl checked for a pulse, but she was dead. No time to drag the brave Officer back to the vehicle. He made his way back to the car just as the gunshots started to ring out and that's when he heard it. The sound of a helicopter and a chance of escape.

Livin' on a prayer

Bon Jovi

Woah, we're half way there
Woah, livin' on a prayer
Take my hand, we'll make it I swear
Woah, livin' on a prayer

36

Chapter

Never had Carl been so pleased to hear the familiar thrum of helicopter rotor blades. He hurriedly made his way back to the Golf. Jenni and the police officer were poised ready to escape, but now the gunshots were coming thick and fast. Brian's police officer looked across at Carl.

'Officer Courtney?' he asked, already shaking his head.

'She didn't make it.' There was no time for sentiment. There was a whooshing noise from above as the helicopter fired an RPG at the Land Rover behind them. it exploded, bursting into flames. It then circled and as it began its descent and then landed on the adjacent field. Jenni managed to get Brian and the police officers grouped behind the car. Swathes of smoke and the acrid smell of burning filled their nostrils, everyone was coughing. Brian sounded like he was choking. Decisions needed to be made and fast. Who was going to make a run for it and who would stay to cover them? Carl could see the Crytex men beginning to edge towards them, passed the burning police car. Now was the time to act. As he was catching his breath, one of the ARV officers decided for them.

190

'You three go. Take Officer Jennings with you. We'll stay and cover you. Our remit was to rescue Brian and you two and get you back to MI5. That's why they sent the helicopter. We have assault rifles stored in the boot of the vehicles. Now go!' There was no time to argue. Carl grabbed Brian around the waist, he had long since pulled out the two drips. Jenni supported Officer Jennings and stumbled across the hard shoulder and along the field as quickly as they could.

The ARV officers had located their machine guns and grenades and were doing them proud, holding off the Crytex thugs. There was no time to watch the shoot-out. The wind created by the helicopter rotor blades made them hold on to each other tightly and they crouched down as they approached. Two Special Forces Agents were leaning out, one with outstretched arms ready to help them on board and one with a machine gun, he was firing on the Crytex men who were now racing towards the helicopter. As they flew over the site, they saw clouds of furling smoke and bodies littering the ground. Jenni said a silent prayer of thanks as Carl pointed toward the flashing blue lights of police vehicles, which were now speeding towards the site in support of their brothers in arms.

'We were lucky they didn't have RPGs.' Carl shouted over the noise of the engine. Brian shrugged his shoulders. 'Rocket-propelled grenades.' he added as Jenni nodded in agreement. 'You were just bloody lucky to get out of there.' One of the armed ARV officers said loudly, as he patted Officer Jennings on the shoulder.

The helicopter was soon out of sight of the raging battlefield and within a few minutes they were approaching Manchester Airport. They came down on a secure landing site and were greeted by military vehicles and several police cars, all with their lights flashing. It was a smooth landing and before the rotor blades had even stopped turning, they were escorted to one of the larger military vehicles and hurriedly pushed inside. The convoy of vehicles departed at speed and within twenty minutes they arrived at a Military Intelligence Barracks on the outskirts of Manchester. On arrival, the police officer was taken away for treatment, but despite Brian's weakened condition he refused to leave Jenni and Carl. It was understandable after such a traumatic experience, a doctor agreed to come to check on Brian. She checked his vitals, and told them all to push fluids, eat something, and to 'take it easy'. They met the first two recommendations but the third was to prove almost impossible. Without Brian, the leaders of Crytex may become desperate and even more dangerous.

It took time to calm down and try to absorb the last twenty-four hours. Hot food and cups of sweet tea helped things come back into focus. After a wash and brush up, the two agents were on the road to recovery. Brian was still in shock and not just from the kidnap, his body needed to withdraw from the drugs that had paralysed him for so many days. But at least they were located in a single, safe and secure location, the inevitable debrief could begin. Due to protocol, they were separated for individual debriefing. The sessions were delivered by experienced officers from MI5 for Jenni, the CIA for

Carl, and Experenta (the owners of the *Watcher 22* program) for Brian. Although the level of the debriefing was slightly different for all three, the questions they were asked were the same. An explanation of what had taken place, a brief assessment of the various incidents, safety and security issues, identifying the captors and lastly assessing the future threat and risk. The questions were different for all three regarding contacts, observations and risk assessment. Brian could only give a limited response as he had been drugged and blindfolded for most of his incarceration. Jenni and Carl were highly trained in observation and situational awareness. They were able to identify the captors from the database and also comment on the operational response. The debriefs were recorded and detailed notes were taken.

After what seemed like hours, they were finally reunited in the secure room, guarded by two armed officers in military uniform. The officers never spoke or lifted their gaze as Brian sat in between Jenni and Carl. His shoulder leaning against Jenni's, it was hardly surprising that he needed reassurance. He was so relieved to see his two rescuers again, but exhaustion was kicking in. It had been a very long day for them all. Suddenly, the two guards sprang to attention. More uniformed officers entered the room and they were all escorted to what looked like a boardroom but without windows. Jenni took a quick look around the table and clocked a couple of military officers with a lot of gold braid, a man in a well-tailored navy suit and a man who she suspected was an MI5 agent, but she didn't recognise the woman. Brian did. Before they could even sit down the woman sprang to her feet and launched herself at Brian with the immortal words,

'We thought you were fuckin' dead!' Brian was almost knocked off his feet, but was beaming as he hugged her back.

'It's so good to see you too Shauna.'

So Good to See You

Cheap Trick

Oh, it's so good to see you
I couldn't wait another day
So good to see you
Oh, I hope everyone missed you
You know they want you to stay

37

Chapter

'They would only let one of us come Brian.' Shauna said excitedly. 'So I made sure that I got in first, obviously I had to clear it with Brown.' She was clinging tightly to Brian and could tell that he'd lost weight as his bones were poking through his clothes. The man in the expensive suit gave Brian a nod accompanied by a wry smile.

'Good to be here Brown.' Brian said to him over Shauna's shoulder.

'Who are these two then?' Shauna asked once she had released Brian, but continued to hold his hand. Before Brian could answer one of the big wigs cut in.

'If everyone could just take a seat. This isn't one of those Long Lost Family programmes. I'm sure that I do not need to explain the seriousness or the urgency of the current situation. There is fierce fighting as we speak and sadly some bloodshed. We owe it to all our officers to strike now and to strike hard.'

Everyone quietly took their seats. Introductions were made by Brown. Jenni and Carl were described as 'Special Agents', and Brian and Shauna were referred to as 'Group Members'. The two big wigs were alluded to as 'Military Advisers' and Brown introduced himself as a 'Company Representative'

'Well, that's as clear as mud!' Shauna stated in her usual outspoken manner. The Military Advisers turned to face her, one of them was a little red-cheeked.

'Young lady! If you speak again, you will be removed and not just from the room. Do I make myself clear?'

Brown and Brian were well aware of Shauna's volatile nature. Brian squeezed her hand and gave her a warning glance. Brown simply glared at her, not always a successful deterrent. Brian could feel her foot tapping the floor in irritation.

'Don't retaliate Shauna, not here and not now.' Shauna looked at Brian, noting his thin face and dark-circled eyes. She nodded slowly. She would try her best. Brian could feel the fight going out of her body and for now at least, he knew that she would at least try and stay quiet. Brian patted Shauna's hand reassuringly, he was desperate for her to stay. She was a beacon of hope for him, someone who knew the real Brian before all this madness had started. Shauna owed him this and she knew it.

'We're collating all your Intel and we have sent reinforcements to accompany our men on the ground. For now, the best plan of action is to reunite you with the Six Keys team. Jenni and Carl will remain with you. They are familiar with Crytex mercenaries and have detailed knowledge of their procedures and shared situational awareness. You know by now how ruthless and aggressive this group is, they will stop at nothing to obtain *Watcher 22*. We are desperately trying to ascertain the extent to which they have infiltrated our agency, our systems and our security. A source of major concern.' he paused, clearly infuriated. 'This operation has now been accelerated to a 'critical level of threat' to our national security. I cannot stress how important the next 48 hours will be.' he said shooting Shauna a look of pure disdain. 'You have done impressive work and showed great bravery, especially our civilian friend.' he said giving Brian a nod of approval. 'But we need each one of you to play your part. The experience and knowledge you have acquired are invaluable. All agencies will be pooling resources to halt these dangerous mercenaries and destroy *Watcher 22* once and for all.' he paused. 'Some experts have argued that we should save the program and experiment with it, discover its true capabilities. But it will be destroyed. We will succeed, we must. That's it. Now I will hand you over to the Operatives officer.'

The other highly decorated officer stood up. 'Shortly you will be meeting with the full complement of team Six Keys. They are in transit. This is a secure base and you will be reunited here. They have done their part and are ready to move to the next phase.' he paused and touched his security earpiece. 'I have just been informed that the team has arrived,' Shauna shuffled around excitedly, like a trapped animal keen to break free. 'You will be travelling light but our surveillance teams will be undercover and watching your every move. You must work together and never be complacent, Crytex has its people everywhere. Trust no-one. This is a highly classified operation. We ask a lot of you, but our agencies will support you and work to protect you. You must not arouse any unnecessary suspicion or endanger the public at any time.' he touched the earpiece again. Shauna raised her hand which was met by a raised eyebrow. 'No time for questions. You will be taken to D block to meet the Keys Team and you will receive further instruction there. Good luck, be strong but be careful.'

Everyone stood as the officers left the room. Brown moved across to shake Brian's free hand. 'We're glad you're free Brian. We would of course have liked you to remain here to recover, but the powers that be insisted that the team stay together. You all have a different experience of the *Watcher 22* program and the knowledge that you do have may be invaluable. Barry has most certainly done his homework and the keys and the clues have been specific and well thought through. It was his attempt at keeping Crytex at bay. Your kidnapping didn't come into the equation. He couldn't have known. But who knows, what this final phase will involve. Now let's reunite you with the others. They are all desperate to see you.'

Within minutes they approached D Block under heavily armed guard. Everyone was well aware of the seriousness of the situation. An officer opened the reinforced steel door and in they went. Jenni and Carl were overwhelmed at their welcome and by the noise as Shauna led the whooping and hugging of the Six Key group members. Brian was the star of the show as each team member greeted him and relief spilled from Berni's eyes in tears of pure happiness. So many times they had feared for Brian's life and now to see him stood before them was amazing. Andy gave Brian a man hug with some hearty banging on his scrawny back. But Brian didn't mind, he savoured every moment.

'Helena get over here!' Shauna shouted across, I had been waiting my turn patiently. Brian was a shadow of his former self, but the smile on his face said it all. Tears glinted in his eyes as he reached out to Shauna and to me, with an arm around each of our waists, he turned to look at Berni and Andy.

'I'm home at last.' he said, his voice breaking with raw emotion. Brown remained in the background, even he was a little choked up.

Jenni and Carl felt like gatecrashers at a very private reunion party. Jenni turned away, reminded of her own family who she hadn't seen for some time. Carl sensed her sadness and turned her towards him.

'I'm here.' he said. 'We have each other, for now at least.' As Carl leaned into her and was about to kiss her. The door slammed shut and yet another heavily decorated officer demanded their attention.

'You've had enough time to regroup. Quieten down. Take your seats. It's now time to plan the final phase. You will be accompanied by these two agents Jenni is one of ours and Carl is from across the pond. That's all you need to know.'

Shauna raised her hand, eager to ask about the plan. He turned to look at her.

'I've been briefed about you, Shauna isn't it? You have no power here do you understand? You are a civilian involved in a military operation. Put your hand down and remain silent.'

Everyone turned collectively to watch Shauna's reaction, the officer had lit the touch paper and knew there would be very little self-control left in her tank. Considering the bigger picture was not a quality that Shauna had ever possessed and this became very apparent, very quickly.

Firework

Katy Perry

Cause baby, you're a firework
Come on, show 'em what you're worth
Make 'em go, "Oh, oh, oh"
As you shoot across the sky
Baby, you're a firework

38

Chapter

We all knew that Shauna is an acquired taste, but I think we'd forgotten just how used to her volatile outbursts we had become. Shauna made the classic mistake and reacted instinctively without 'knowing her audience'. Whilst she had successfully manoeuvred her way around the likes of Brown and Cagney and Lacey, the military bigwigs were experienced, professional experts in their field and showed zero tolerance for Shauna's shenanigans.

Following the debrief things went from bad to worse and only by the grace of God and Berni did Shauna remain with us in the meeting room. The main focus of the meeting was on security measures, weaponry, comms and backup plans. But until we had the sixth key and knew the location, the logistics could not be finalised. We were lucky to leave the barracks in one piece. Never mind the threat from Crytex, Shauna was doing a pretty good job of self-sabotage. We managed to get through the meeting and I was just about to issue a sigh of relief as we all headed for the door. It was then that Shauna chose to turn and verbally blast one of the military officers. We manage to restrain her, as she would have faced up to him, she had no fear. The officer in question stood stock still, not afraid of a firecracker like Shauna. With one final lunge forward she suggested where the officer could shove his laser pointer from the presentation. He showed a flush of annoyance and looked as though he could have responded. Fortunately, Lacey and I managed to bundle her through the door and out of the building. Within moments we were back on the road again, our team now complete at long last.

It only took ten minutes for us to be transported to our new hotel location. At least we didn't have to unpack very much, as all we had were toiletries. The purple flash of colour on the exterior of the building and the white moon logo on the purple background, left us in no doubt that we were now staying at a Premier Inn, which suited me perfectly. I never thought that I'd get complacent about staying in hotels. But I did. We all did, all of us except Brian that is. Perhaps we had just stayed at too many. Moving around so much made you feel disoriented and unsettled. I missed Charlie, my partner, of course, but also my home comforts, like privacy and chill-out time. But compared to the horror that Brian had endured, we had nothing to complain about. Cagney and Lacey herded us inside and as usual, an entire floor of the hotel had been cleared for us. Once we had located our rooms and deposited our meagre belongings, we were taken to a small conference room. There was no time to settle in.

'Today the team will all be going out together. Jenni and Carl will stay here with Brown and begin planning the route to Lindisfarne. The team will decipher the next clue. There's no time to lose. Lacey has planned a safe route to the bank and we will follow the normal procedure. Andy and Helena will retrieve the clue and then we will all go to the location.'

Within ten minutes the two Range Rovers were positioned around the corner from the bank. It was a seamless operation. This time Andy and I were quickly in and out. Simon had been briefed and everything went to plan. If we were being watched, it wasn't obvious. We jumped back into the Range Rover and gave the postcode for the location which was The Pankhurst Centre. Lacey phoned ahead, to ensure we could gain access before the Centre opened to the public. We pulled up outside what appeared to be a quite ordinary-looking but large house. On the way, I talked a little about the Suffragette movement and about the women who put their lives at risk and took direct action to secure votes for women. This building was the home of Emmeline Pankhurst and her family who led the Suffragette campaign for Votes for Women. The very place where the first meeting of the Women's Social and Political Union was held. Everyone needed to know a little about the background and their famous motto, 'deeds not words' Words had proved useless in the fight for women's votes Many women were arrested, tried, imprisoned and tortured for their cause. Shauna looked visibly shocked.

'Jesus. I never knew. Not really, not about the suffering. I'll never waste one of my votes again.' I simply nodded at her.

'The bravery of these women changed things forever and I will be eternally grateful.'

'I should know about this! We all should. Why didn't those dip shits at our schools teach us about the suffragettes instead of fractions and French?'

'Did you go to school Shauna?' Andy asked, leaning back to avoid any physical contact.

'That will do you two. Let's show some respect.' Berni looked across at the pair, who were now smiling amicably.

'What does the clue say?' I asked and Andy read it aloud.

'The clue is just a short poem - let me read it before we go in.

Will you walk into the parlour?" said the Spider to the Fly,

It is the most important parlour that ever you did spy;

And at the table where they sat, when planning daring deeds

Is the photograph of Jasmine, you'll need her to proceed.'

'Jesus let's hope that makes more sense once we're in there.'

The Pankhurst Centre is run by volunteers and as the team walked up the path, one of the volunteers, Rachel, opened the door to let us in.

'We need to find the parlour.' Shauna told Rachel as they entered the hallway. It was wonderful if not a little overwhelming to be in the Pankhurst house.

'Follow me.' Rachel said in a business-like tone. 'I've been instructed to assist with anything you need.' Shauna kept stopping to look at the photographs that lined the walls. Berni felt overcome by a mixture of pride and emotion, knowing what these women had sacrificed for the good of others.

'This is the parlour.' Rachel said as they descended the staircase into a lovely room, with a piano on one side and glorious bay windows that stretched down to the floor. In front of the windows was an Edwardian table and chairs, the table had a circle of glass on top of it and there were documents under the glass and a magnifying glass to hand.

'Is this where they had their meetings? I mean for planning their deeds and actions?' Andy asked.

'As far as we know the meetings took place here in the parlour and at this very table.' Rachel said proudly.

'Could we move the chairs and look at the documents?'

'You may, but carefully.' Rachel moved two of the chairs to one side as the team moved forward.

'Can I ask what you are looking for?'

'It's a photograph, we have to find a photograph of Jasmine.'

It was hard not to be distracted by the historical documents which were protected under the piece of glass. Such important work had been carried out here. The team moved around the table and Rachel used the magnifying glass to get a closer look.

'Everything looks in order, I don't see anything unusual or a photograph.'

'Can we remove the glass cover, Rachel? We must find the photograph of Jasmine.' Rachel hesitated.

'I'll need to get Margery involved. Could you wait a moment?' Rachel left the room and within minutes returned with Margery in tow. Margery looked a little flustered. but after straightening her floral blouse and putting her reading glasses up on her head, she took a long look at the group. Thankfully Shauna kept stum. Margery nodded and agreed that the glass could be removed.

'It will take four of us. It isn't heavy but it's awkward to lift. If we can have the two strapping men, one on each side.' Margery pointed to Lacey and Andy. Brian tried not to look hurt but was aware of his frail appearance and felt relieved that he did not have to exert himself. Shauna and I stood back. This would be a delicate operation. The glass was lifted gently from the table and as it did so one of the documents fluttered to the ground. Rachel and Margery looked understandably distressed.

'I'll get it, don't worry.' Berni said as she bent over to pick up the precious document. And that was when Berni saw the passport-sized photograph. It must have been hidden underneath the document.

'I have it!' Berni said excitedly. 'Now all we have to do is find Jasmine.'

Picture this

Blondie

All I want is a photo in my wallet
A small remembrance of something more solid
All I want is a picture of you

'It's a good job Barry's already dead!' Shauna said, as Margery and Rachel carefully realigned the precious documents before Andy and Lacey lifted the piece of glass back onto the table, both of the volunteers looked suitably relieved.

'Why did he have to make it so damn hard! Barry's such a dick!'

'Thank you for that Shauna.' Andy said shaking his head, duly noting the look of disapproval on the faces of the volunteers.

'He could just have asked Margery to keep the photo in her drawer.' Shauna continued, clearly revving up for one of her tirades.

'He made it difficult Shauna because Crytex are always right behind us, they are extremely dangerous and Barry knew it.' Brian nodded in agreement, he knew it too.

'If it had just been straightforward, Crytex would have taken possession of *Watcher 22* by now and the history and possibly the future of the world would be at risk.'

'Yeah yeah. I get all that Helena. But he's still a ...'

'Yes, thank you Shauna.' Berni interrupted quickly. The volunteers did not deserve to hear any more of Shauna's colourful descriptions.

'We need to focus now on the photograph. The group clamoured round and Berni signalled for Margery and Rachel to come forward in case they recognised Jasmine.

Alas, no one recognised the lady with long black hair with an aquiline nose and beautiful blue eyes who stared back at them from the photograph.

'She's a stunner alright.'

'Thank you, Andy.' Shauna snapped back at him. 'Probably one of Barry's conquests. We know he couldn't keep it in his pants.'

'Shauna show some respect. Kindly remember where we are!' Berni was not amused. Margery coughed in disapproval, but Rachel was struggling to disguise a smile.

'What are we supposed to do now? It's no use having a chuffin' photo without some idea of what to do with it.'

'Hold on Shauna. Let's just take a moment.' Andy said as he deftly turned the photograph over. And there it was in pencil. Faint but legible. You'll find me at the place where Christabel studied. Margery and Rachel both sprang back from the group simultaneously.

'Christabel Pankhurst was a graduate in law from The University of Manchester.' Margery said with pride in her voice. Rachel nodded and smiled, pleased that Margery had her moment.

'That's brilliant. Thank you, Margery.' Berni said flashing a winning smile.

'The University of Manchester is very close by. But I don't think we should all go. You've both been so helpful and we can't thank you enough.' I turned towards the two volunteers.

'Hang on there Helena. We need to ask something first. Do either of you have any connections to the University, before we decide who's going over there?'

'Before you answer it's only right you should know that it could be dangerous. We may be followed and you may be putting yourselves in harm's way.' I added, determined that the volunteers knew something of the risk involved.

'Now I should remind you where we are, we are in the meeting room in the Pankhurst house.' Margery said calmly. 'Do you think that any of these women would have faltered and what's more…'

'I should go.' Rachel interrupted. 'Someone needs to stay here and open our Centre to the public.' Rachel gave Margery a reassuring nod. 'I understand the urgency of the situation, but more importantly, I know one of the receptionists, a chap named Will. The University won't give out staff details to just anyone and by the time you have the paperwork in place, Crytex may have caught up with us.' Margery looked relieved. She had helped in the best way she could, but she was happy to leave the next part of the adventure to Rachel. After a short discussion, it was decided that Rachel would head up the team accompanied by Berni, Lacey and Andy. Cagney would take me, Brian and Shauna back to the Premier Inn. Too many people asking questions would just arouse even more suspicion. We headed back to the Land Rover whilst the other team set off on foot.

Rachel was true to her word and after entering the campus she asked Lacey to accompany her to the reception desk. Although she had been a student at the University and kept in touch with staff and colleagues, asking about staff members would need a more formal approach. Initially, Will refused to give them any information, but once Lacey flashed his ID, he agreed to check with his manager. No one could contest MI5 ID and they soon had the information that they needed. They were told that Jasmine was working in the Manchester Museum. Lacey stressed that Jasmine was not under suspicion or wanted by the police, it was merely her help that they needed. Before they set off, Lacey quickly checked in with Cagney using his earpiece and buttonhole microphone. This was standard procedure, updating each other with any developments or changes in location. As the Museum was a public place, it would be easily accessible to the Crytex hunters. Fortunately, Manchester Museum is part of the University of Manchester campus. Rachel and Lacey took the lead and Berni and Andy walked behind them, linking arms. They knew that they may be under surveillance and Lacey was on high alert. Meanwhile, Rachel gave them a little background about the museum and its history.

'Manchester Museum is owned by the University of Manchester and was opened in 1887. Remarkably it's the home of approximately four and a half million objects. In February this year, there was a much-needed refurbishment. The idea behind it is to build new relationships with communities across the world.'

'It does sound like the kind of thing Barry would have been interested in.'

'I agree Andy and look at the building, it's simply marvellous.' Berni was in awe of the Gothic architecture.

Within minutes they were inside the museum and Rachel and Lacey repeated their spiel to the museum receptionists. Luckily there were two receptionists on duty, one of whom offered to take them straight to Jasmine who was working on the top floor in an office near the fossils and dinosaurs gallery. If Lacey was excited about coming face to face with prehistoric giants such as the Tyrannosaurus Rex and Tenontosaurus, he didn't show it. Berni and Andy agreed to wait at reception and keep their eyes peeled for any dubious visitors. It was very busy, the new Egyptian collection being a key attraction.

Just before their team members left, Berni had 'one of her turns', as Shauna always called them. The other receptionist got her a seat.

'What is it Berni?'

'I'm not sure. But I do know that we need to get out of here. I think it might be the others who are in danger.' Lacey called Cagney and plans were put in place for immediate relocation. Berni's instinct had never been wrong before.

'We need to find Jasmine, Rachel will you join us? Andy can you stay with Berni, just sit behind reception. We'll be as fast as we can.' Andy gave Berni the bottle of water kindly provided by one of the receptionists.

'We don't have long Andy. The threat is close and very real. I'm worried about the others. I think Crytex may have found them.'

The Climb

Joe McElderry

There's always gonna be another mountain
I'm always gonna wanna make it move
Always gonna be an uphill battle
Sometimes I'm gonna have to lose
Ain't about how fast I get there
Ain't about what's waiting on the other side
It's the climb

40

Chapter

It felt as though we were hurtling into the unknown. No one liked the team being split up and by rescuing Brian we had succeeded in making the Crytex hunters angry and even more dangerous.

Whilst the other half of our team located Jasmine, we were in the Land Rover heading back to the Premier Inn. Cagney was unsettled and seemed to be checking the front mirror a little too often. He messed with his earpiece and then said something that I couldn't hear properly, I felt sure the word backup was mentioned. I looked to my friends to see if they had noticed anything, but Shauna was just babbling away next to me and Brian was falling asleep. We stopped at the traffic lights and Cagney went into the right-hand lane and indicated right, but uncharacteristically he kept revving the engine and I noticed that the hand brake was off. That's when it happened. The car tyres screeched as Cagney pulled out very fast and cut across the inside lane, in front of another car. Fortunately, the driver in the car we cut up managed to slam on his brakes. It was close, very close, a desperate measure. The noise of the beeping car horns roused Brian and the rather graphic hand gestures elicited a response from Shauna that would make an experienced truck driver blush. Now everyone in the car was on high alert and Cagney was speaking loudly asking for directions. He then turned to us.

'Hold on tight, check your seat belts are secure. We're being followed. But backup is on the way, Jenni and Carl have been despatched to collect the other team from the museum....' Cagney paused as he took another sharp left at speed down a grimy backstreet. He was taking instruction through the earpiece. Even Shauna stayed silent. We took another left and shot through a traffic light on amber. All the while Cagney was checking the front mirror. His final flourish as we approached Piccadilly Station was to overtake a parked car. We missed the oncoming bus by about a centimetre.

'Fuckin' hell Cagney! Are you trying to kill us all? Brian's already had a near-death experience.'

'Not now Shauna.' I said as I squeezed Shauna's arm and gave her a knowing look. The car came to a sudden stop outside Piccadilly Station. Cagney barked out the instructions.

'Go into the station, ask at the ticket office for eight tickets to Sheffield, the fast train, not the one that takes an hour. I'll park the car and meet you inside. Talk to no one. Move!'

We didn't need telling twice. Shauna and I got out first and then helped Brian who was visibly shaken, it had been a long day for him. As soon as we had slammed the doors shut, Cagney sped off. We linked arms and put Brian in the middle to give him support. The station was very busy. We made our way passed the 'Victory Over Blindness' statues which depict seven blinded First

World War soldiers leading one another away from the battlefield with their hands on the shoulder of the man in front. Very powerful, but not the time to stop and look. We seated Brian on one of the plastic chairs just inside the entrance.

'You stay with him Shauna, I'll get the tickets.' Brian was much too shaky to be left alone and Shauna would have made her presence known if there was even the slightest problem when purchasing the tickets. I was not a lover of ticket machines and was certainly not in the right frame of mind to be messing around with them today. I took Brian's advice and headed for the ticket office. Thankfully, there was only a small queue. I took a deep breath, did a quick visual check on Shauna and Brian and focused on trying not to look as shaky as I felt. After a short wait that felt like forever, I was at the head of the queue. It only took a few moments to pay for the eight single tickets. Cagney was right the faster train only took 50 minutes unlike the 'Sheffield chuffer' which took over an hour and it stopped a lot at handsomely named places such as Grindleford and Hathersage. Sadly this was not a day for sightseeing or enjoying the breathtaking views of Edale.

I knew that there were ticket barriers in place which meant that we would have to wait for everyone to arrive and go through together. The next fast train was not for another thirty minutes which would give the others time to join us. I walked back across the station to sit with Brian and Shauna, guessing that it wouldn't be long until Shauna got itchy feet, I was right.

'I think we need some strong coffee with sugar and maybe a snack for Brian.' Shauna said anxiously. To be fair Brian was very pale. 'I've seen a Starbucks and it's close by. You two stay here and I'll nip over and get the drinks.'

'Best get one for Cagney. He looks like a double espresso man to me. Now Shauna, please just go straight there and back. Don't talk to anyone or draw attention to yourself.' Shauna smiled.

'I'm not ten years old Helena for fucks sake!'

'Remember the Crytex hunters may be staking out the station, I don't think they will have followed us here as yet, after Cagney's...'

'After Cagney's what?' I jumped, Cagney had come up behind me.

'Erm, I was just saying how your expert driving took us out of any immediate danger.'

'Crazy bastard!'

Cagney bumped Shauna on the arm in a friendly way.

'You're alive, aren't you? And not kidnapped or tortured or drugged.'

'You'll get no argument from me.' Brian said quietly.

'Shauna, perhaps you and I should go and get the drinks. Cagney can keep an eye on Brian now and look out for the others.'

'Good idea. Brian may be able to recognise some of the Crytex men and this location close to the door is ideal. Double espresso and a sandwich for me please.'

Shauna released a tiny snort and I dragged her away before she could do any more damage.

We decided to buy a range of goodies and a selection of teas and coffees in preparation for our friends' arrival. This was a good move as the other team had arrived when we got back and were standing with Cagney and Brian. We welcomed Jasmine who looked nervous, we then said our hellos to the other group members and gave out hugs to those who needed them. Everyone shared the spoils amicably. This wasn't the place to ask Jasmine any questions, but she was carrying a rather handsome briefcase which was also attached to her wrist with a strap. The documents it contained must be very important. Jenni and Carl took their drinks with them as they went out on patrol. They both had surveillance experience and were also familiar with Maxim and Loopy Lars. Cagney and Lacey guarded us discreetly and they were obviously in close contact with HQ. I gave out the tickets. In such a volatile situation, everyone needed to have their own ticket in case we got split up.

'I think we should stay in smaller groups. A large group attracts attention. We need to make our way over to platform 7. Cagney, could you take your group first.'

Within minutes we were all safely on the platform and we stayed in our assigned groups. We didn't know where Jenni and Carl were exactly, but we knew they were watching out for us. The familiar nasal message came over the station tannoy and we were readying ourselves to board the train. That's when something strange happened, something unexpected, and something that would change things.

Midnight Train to Georgia

Gladys Knight & the Pips

He's leaving (leaving)
On that midnight train to Georgia (leaving on a midnight train)
Hmm, yeah
Said he's going back (going back to find)
To a simpler place and time (and when he takes that ride)
Oh yes, he is (guess who's gonna sit right by his side)

41

Chapter

We had just started queuing to board the train when it happened. Jenni and Carl were running down the platform toward us, at a great pace. Everyone felt tense and Brian looked terrified.

'Stand your ground. Don't attract any undue attention. Perhaps they have a lead about one of the passengers.' We all tried to remain calm, but Brian was panicking. It was hard not to. I knew so little about this world of espionage with its car chases, helicopters and drones, but I was catching up. Cagney took up a protective stance behind us. I looked around trying to glean any tell-tale signs from the faces of the other passengers. They looked tired and weary just as we did, fatigued by the continuous commute. Jenni and Carl increased their speed to a run. Something was wrong, very wrong. Had Crytex tracked us already? We had no phones, no devices and the cars had been ditched. There was of course CCTV at the station which could have been hacked, but this was a very public space. Surely they wouldn't try something here?

Jenni and Carl ran past our group, heading further down the platform. That's when it happened. Brown suddenly stepped back from his group and began running in the opposite direction. And of course, that's when the train doors opened. Cagney hurried us onto the train. Lacey did the same with his group. For safety reasons, the groups were in separate carriages. We were fortunate in securing seats opposite each other, with a table in the middle.

'What the fuck is going on Cagney?' Shauna said with her usual tact.

Cagney shook his head, before putting his finger to his earpiece.

'Stay here.' he stood up and made his way passed the busy commuters and entered the other carriage.

'Helena, you don't think Brown has turned traitor do you?

Brian shook his head in answer.

'He's been with us from the start, loyal to our team throughout. It must be a mix-up of some sort.' Brian laid his head back on the supporting cushion, he was exhausted. The beeping of the door locks indicated our departure. Three of our team were not on the train and who knew if anyone from Crytex was on board. Cagney returned and even for him his face looked a little pale.

'I know you all want to know what's happened with Brown.' he lowered his voice when he said his name. Not a great sign. Cagney looked carefully around the train.

'All I can say is that the worst thing that could happen has happened. I don't know all the details but we must push on without him, for now at least. Crytex are grade one manipulators and he could be the victim of blackmail or some other serious threat.'

'Bastard, what a ...'

'That's enough Shauna. Not here and not now, understood.'

'There's no evidence is there Cagney?' Brian asked with his eyes half closed.

'Brian is correct. Innocent until proven guilty and all that. There is one thing though and it was flagged a few days ago, Crytex seems to have been one step ahead of us all the way, even after Brian was rescued.' I nodded.

'And let's not forget that he ran. I've never seen Brown run before.'

Everyone at our table went quiet. It was a massive shock. If Brown hadn't run I would have defended him to the hilt. He had guided us all through the *Watcher 22* program and although he could be pompous and irritating, there was no way any of us would have suspected him of this.

'For now, we focus on staying together and staying safe. If Brown has been leaking information or carrying a tracker, Crytex most likely knows not only where we are, but also where we are going. So things may change very quickly. You need to be ready to move at a moment's notice. Jasmine is struggling with the situation, but fortunately, Berni is a calming influence. We don't know the facts yet and therefore we mustn't judge. Our job is clear, we need to find a safe house, collate all the clues and information and then, after some rest, we move forward. We are two agents down for now so I would ask that you all remain observant and Brian if you see anyone at all that you suspect, you must say so. We have asked for reinforcements and they should be meeting us at Sheffield. Maxim and Lars may be in disguise, although I think they may have avoided the train. My feeling is that they will be making their own way to Sheffield.'

'Jesus Christ Cagney! I could wring Barry's neck!'

'I'm sure he didn't realise...'

'Well, I'm sure he fuckin' did realise. Putting his own life at risk was one thing but dragging us all into this warped Agatha Christie shite is something else and we all know it.'

'I feel sorry for Jasmine. At least we all volunteered for the *Watcher* 22 program. Jasmine was just minding her own business and then she gets thrown into this chaotic adventure...'

'We're not the bleedin' famous five Helena. I wouldn't call this an adventure, it lost the right to be described as an adventure when they kidnapped Brian.'

'For once Shauna I agree. I wasn't belittling Brian's horrendous ordeal. It's very difficult to believe what's happening,'

'Well let's hope Jasmine is wearing her big girl pants because things are not going to calm down.'

'I agree Shauna and it must be such a shock being thrust into our crazy world. One minute you are working at the museum and the next you are on a train with MI5 agents and a crazy team of people, heading for Sheffield to try and destroy a program you didn't even know existed.'

Shauna nodded, I looked over at Brian but he was sleeping the sleep of the exhausted, with his mouth slightly open and his head lolled to one side. Maybe he shouldn't have pushed himself to come along, but he insisted and anyway, there isn't really anywhere that's safe from Crytex. As we pulled into Stockport station,

Cagney stood up. He held his earpiece and spoke quietly, before turning toward us.

'We have some backup. If you think that you've clocked one of them, do not stare or arouse attention in any way, did you hear me, Shauna?'

Shauna shot him a look of pure loathing, fortunately, he was too distracted to notice.

We had never seen Cagney and Lacey working as agents in the field before. They had always been our drivers, escorts and security guards. The veneer of politeness was now stripped back and we could only observe and admire their expertise. Well I could, but then there was Shauna. Her foot was already tapping. She couldn't resist leaning over the sleeping Brian to get a better view out of the window.

'Shauna for God's sake, sit back down.' She reluctantly obeyed. Once the doors had closed Cagney returned to his seat.

'Well, where are they then? Where's the bleedin' backup? We have Crytex hunters tracking our every move!' Cagney leaned towards her and gave her direct eye contact, the kind I would imagine you would encounter in an interrogation.

'This is your last warning. You are under our jurisdiction. Don't look around. Don't mention the name of the company. Don't draw attention to yourself and…'

'Don't fuckin' patronise me.! Don't speak down to me and don't ever look at me like that again! I know the rule of three when giving instructions.' Shauna said through gritted teeth. 'Now if you don't mind I need to visit the ladies. Do you want to come with me or can I be trusted?'

Cagney waved his hand in a dismissive gesture and looked out of the window.

Shauna was not one to take instruction lightly, often spiralling in the opposite direction especially if it was targeted solely at her. Therefore I was not at all surprised when ten minutes later, a rather flustered Shauna was being accompanied back to her seat by an elderly gentleman wearing a tweed flat cap and nondescript raincoat. If he was a member of the backup team he fitted in perfectly, that is when he wasn't escorting nosy women back to their seats. The elderly chap leaned across the table and whispered something to Cagney before leaving the carriage. Shauna looked suitably ashamed.

'Stay in your seat, keep your mouth shut, and do as I ask. That's my rule of three.'

'I only wanted to see Andy and Berni…'

'You know that carriage is off limits. Stay put. The next stop is Sheffield and it could get hairy. Cagney put his hand to his ear. 'Crytex hunters are already at the station. We have a plan and all of you need to listen.'

I'm still standing

Elton John

Don't you know I'm still standin', better than I ever did.
Lookin' like a true survivor,
feelin' like a little kid.
And I'm still standin', after all this time.
Picking up the pieces of my life without you on my mind.

42

Chapter

Everyone who knew Shauna, also knew that listening was not one of her greatest accomplishments. In fairness, she did try but could not seem to refrain from butting in. But Cagney's plan involved everyone and he was determined to deliver it uninterrupted.

'You can ask questions when I've finished.' Cagney said, shooting Shauna yet another warning glance. 'In fifteen minutes we will arrive at Sheffield train station. As I said previously, we believe that Crytex will have its people watching us as we leave the train. We do have a safe house prepared as we can't risk staying at any of the hotels. Have no doubt, we will be followed. We think our only chance is to split up which will confuse them. However...'

Cagney held up his hand to silence Shauna. She had moved to the edge of her seat with her elbows perched on the table, a sign she was ready to interrupt. Cagney pushed on. 'As we know what their game plan will be, we have the opportunity to create a diversion. We don't think Crytex knows exactly how many of us there are, which gives us an advantage. They are familiar with Helena and Andy from their visits to the bank and obviously, they know Brian.' Brian sat up with a start.

225

Again Cagney raised his hand. 'Let me finish. We don't want our three key team members followed to the safe house or captured. Our plan is simple, we want Jasmine, Brian, Berni and Andy, together with our agent, to go straight to the safe house. They will be known as Team S, as in safe house. To achieve this, we need to create a diversion. We believe that Crytex will be looking out for team members that they know and recognise.' I could feel Shauna tapping her foot and wriggling around impatiently. 'Lacey is about the same build as Brian and I think I can pass for Andy. So we have decided that we will exchange clothes and hope that in the heat of the moment, they will follow us and give Team S a chance to get away. We will be known as Team D - for decoy. Hopefully, they'll take the bait. That's the first part of the plan.' Cagney paused and that was his mistake.

Shauna was straight in, 'Bollocks Cagney! Crytex knows we are a bigger team than that! They won't go for it, not with just two of you. There's only one solution and you know it!' Cagney looked down at his shoes. You could tell that he did know. But even I wasn't expecting what came next. 'You two play dress up and you might get away with impersonating Andy and Brian, but it's unlikely. They know Helena and would recognise her from the bank trips and I'm pretty sure they've clocked me by now. You know what I think? I think that you know damn well that we have to come with you.' she paused. 'We stay dressed as we are now and that will lure the Crytex bastards to follow us and let Team S escape.' There was a rare moment of silence.

'She's right of course.' Brian said looking around the group as he collected nods of agreement.

'You will be putting yourselves at risk. That's why we didn't ask you. Plus we know that they will recognise Helena. We were going to take Andy instead of Shauna, but we thought...'

'Go on fuckin' say it, you thought I would stand out, be an obvious target. Cheeky sod.' Cagney sensibly did not counter and averted his eyes and took a different tack.

'The loss of Brown has changed the dynamic. We stand a chance of success if this new plan works.'

'Well, it's decided then.' Shauna turned to look at me and raised her eyebrows and hands, posing the question.

'I don't think we have a choice. At least Team S will get away safely and we will have Cagney and Lacey to protect us, what could go wrong.'

'Don't underestimate the danger you will be putting yourselves in. If they catch one of us, you know from Brian's treatment that it's brutal and they are even more desperate now. Is everyone clear? Team S is Andy, Brian, Berni and Jasmine escorted by one of our agents to the safe house. Team D will consist of me, Lacey, Shauna and Helena.' Everyone nodded.

'We don't have much time left, so let me be the first one to say it Cagney, isn't it time you got your kit off!' Everyone laughed, Shauna was irrepressible.

As we approached Sheffield station the teams were assembled in separate carriages and suitably attired. Lacey had joined us and was now dressed as Brian and Cagney looked quite fetching in Andy's jacket and scarf. The elderly agent we had seen earlier, would now escort Team S from their carriage to the safe house. Since we had lost not only Brown but Jenni and Carl, this new plan carried risks for both teams. But here we sat, Shauna bubbling with excitement, Cagney and Lacey bracing themselves and then there was me, just hoping that I would keep up, my running days were in the dim and distant past, if they had ever existed at all.

'Link me.' Cagney said to Shauna as we were all standing by the train door ready to exit.

'You know how to impress a girl don't you.' Shauna was quite giddy with excitement.

'Focus Shauna. We are leaving the carriage before Team S, they will hang back and hopefully Crytex will follow us.'

Lacey turned to me. 'You might want to hold my hand, Helena?'

Shauna did her mocking voice giving a good imitation of Lacey's voice. I think it was the nerves that made me giggle. We descended the carriage and headed for the ticket turnstile. 'Remember you can look scared and turn around a few times. We need to make it look as though we are trying not to be followed when the opposite is true. We're lucky that Shauna naturally attracts attention.' Lacey said with a smile. I could hear the sound of my heart pounding in my head as we approached the turnstile.

'I think we've got one of them following us, just behind on the left. You can look at them, remember our aim is to be followed.' I turned and caught the eye of a blonde-haired man, whose face had pockmarks and whose pockets seemed abnormally bulky. Could this be Maxim, the Russian kidnapper that Brian had told us about? This was duly confirmed as we passed through the turnstile as just beyond the plastic seating area, there was another man hopping excitedly from one foot to the other. He was looking straight at the man behind us and started walking toward the turnstile.

'Shit, that's Lars.' Lacey said under his breath. 'He'll block our exit.' Lacey spoke quietly into his coat microphone.

'Time for British Rail to come to our assistance in the 'search for the lost tickets.' distraction. We shall not pass, not without the tickets.'

Cagney played his part perfectly and all four of us were escorted to the ticket office, rightfully reprimanded for travelling without a ticket and made to purchase replacement tickets. The Crytex men would not be cocky enough to apprehend us in the busy ticket office, not with so many rail staff around. Cagney clocked the station manager and took him to one side. Within minutes we were taken to one of the Staff Mess Rooms which are not accessible to the public and fortunately for us it, it had two doors. We swept straight through the staff room. Cagney must have pulled the MI5 card and moments later we were running through Sheffield train station with two mad Crytex agents on our tail.

'Get in the first taxi.' Cagney shouted to the others as he flashed his badge. It felt awkward barging to the front of the queue and stealing the first taxi. But this was nothing compared to what Lars and Maxim did. Hot on our tail, they didn't hesitate. They also ran to the front of the taxi rank, pushing men, women and children aside, an old lady was knocked to the floor. Only one young man stepped forward to try and protest and he was punched in the face for his trouble. No one dared intervene after that. And then we had a stroke of luck, as the taxi departed. Our taxi driver swore under his breath.

'Looks like those buggers got what they deserve. Scumbags.'

It had taken a policeman, a train guard and a taxi driver to prevent Lars and Maxim from following us. But that didn't mean we were safe. Lacey told the driver to take us on the scenic route before arriving at the hotel.

'That was fuckin' awesome !'

'It's not over yet Shauna.' Lacey said quietly. 'Crytex is a massive international operation. More will come.' How right he was.

Where the Streets Have No Name

U2

I want to run, I want to hide
I wanna tear down the walls that hold me inside
I wanna reach out and touch the flame
Where the streets have no name, ha, ha, ha

43

Chapter

After a scenic taxi ride around Sheffield, we finally arrived at a rather swanky hotel, the Mercure St Paul's Hotel and Spa to be precise. As we pulled up Shauna said what I was thinking, 'We're not really staying here, are we? You're just fuckin' playing with us.'

'No Shauna, we're playing with them. That's what we're doing. So if you could just button it. Our target is to rejoin Team S without leading Crytex to the safe house.'

'Could you fill us in with some of the details Cagney?' I asked gently. 'You see if we suddenly have to take off, I may be a little slower than you three.'

'No one knows how this will play out. I have ordered afternoon tea for us all. With a bit of luck, we will have time to eat it. And no Shauna we will not be staying here, but if they are tracking us, Crytex may think we are. In theory, Maxim and Lars will be delayed at the station and have lost the trail.'

Ten minutes later we were all sat in comfy chairs under a canopy of lights in the glorious atrium. The stunning glass walls and ceilings overlooked the Millennium

Gallery. It was a sight to behold with the green foliage and wonderful plants. But should we be relaxing, surely they'd find us here? Cagney had wandered off and was making contact with HQ. Then, just as were about to begin eating the lovely scones, Lacey went very pale and suddenly stood up.

'I think I know how they are tracking us. I kept wondering how they seem to know our every move, even moves that Brown couldn't have told them about. We change the itinerary almost hourly, even though we aren't always sure of our next steps.' with that Lacey removed his coat, well Brian's coat to be exact, before sitting down again.

'It must be this damn coat, it has to be.' Lacey began his search of the coat, checking the pockets. Nothing. Next, he deftly checked the buttons and both lapels. Nada. He persevered, running his fingers along the hem and the coat lining. Then he stopped dead. He had found something. It was a small black tracker. It had been tucked inside the hem of Brian's coat and was about the size of a five-pence piece. Lacey sprang into action. He stood up, threw the coat onto the chair and ran to the exit. Cagney returned to the group and we knew then that we would not be eating the rest of the cakes and fancies.

Lacey was completely out of breath when he returned. Later we learned that he'd thrown the tracker into the back of an Amazon delivery truck whilst the driver was busy delivering parcels. But Crytex would know about our visit to the hotel and it was time to go. Cagney had paid the bill on arrival and now we had to move and quickly.

'Don't arouse suspicion. Walk calmly. Follow me.' Cagney opened the glass door that lead into the beautiful Millennium Gallery. It was just coats on and a brisk stroll through this wondrous glasshouse with its superb display of plants, before we had to run again. Cagney had asked the taxi driver to double back after he had dropped us off and paid him to wait outside the Millennium Gallery exit. Thankfully, he was true to his word. After the brisk walk, we ran to the taxi, which was parked just across the road and we were on our way. Cagney and Lacey looked relieved when we were on the move again. The taxi driver did a thirty-minute detour around the city before Cagney gave him the address of the safe house.

'Don't tell anyone will you, the address I mean.' Shauna leaned forward as she spoke to the taxi driver, who was having a strange day.

'Shauna. Desist. It's all been cleared and prearranged.'

'When will we get to stop driving around Lacey? I'm knackered.'

'Knackered but safe, let's not forget that shall we.'

'When will it all be over though? We've collected the soddin' keys and solved Barry's ridiculous clues. I mean do you even need us for the last bit?'

'Look Shauna, there may be something at the final destination. If we get there and Barry has used some other bizarre clue that only the original team from the Watcher program can solve then where would we be? We need you all there. This is a matter of national security after all.' Cagney said quietly in Shauna's ear.

'Blah blah. I'm fuckin' sick of being shunted from pillar to post, that's all.'

'You would have been properly sick if Crytex had captured and tortured you.' Cagney whispered in her ear. It was never a good idea to go up against Shauna when she felt justified in her complaint. That much I had learned. Small red rosebuds of annoyance began to appear on Shauna's cheeks as she turned to face Cagney head-on. Fortunately, the taxi took a sharp left-hand turn which threw us all around in the back of the black cab. Perhaps the driver could sense the tension, he did take it rather hard.

'Jesus Christ driver, you know we're not strapped in right?'

'That's hardly his fault Shauna.' I gave her a look as we pulled on our seat belts.

'There is a sign back there young lady, with clear instructions.'

'It's a right turn just passed the phone box.' Lacey interrupted.

'Just ten more minutes Shauna. Do you think you can contain yourself for that long?'

Shauna glared back at him and muttered an obscenity under her breath that definitely wasn't 'banker' but rhymed with it. Luckily, I was the only one to catch it.

Ten minutes later we pulled up at a beautiful stone cottage with a concealed drive, which again our driver took at speed. I opened the door of the taxi and stepped onto the stone driveway, the surrounding garden was beautiful. Shauna tumbled out first just as the back door of the cottage opened and Berni and Andy bounded towards us. There was much hugging and banter. Even Brian managed to join in accompanied by Jasmine. Long after the taxi left, when we were all sitting around a real fire sipping hot tea and eating hearty ham muffins, only then did some sense of relief wash over us. Cagney stood guard outside. The local police were doing regular drive-bys. For now at least we felt some sense of safety. I looked over at Jasmine, her face was pale and drawn and she was still attached to the briefcase. I was about to reach out to her when Mouthy started again.

'What now Lacey? Do we get some bloody sleep? There are beds here right?'

Berni sighed. 'There are bunk beds, space enough for us all and they seem comfortable enough.'

'Are we in the Brownies? Come on guys, you should have seen the beautiful hotel we just had to leave...'

'You're not on holiday Shauna. This is serious. We have to get this right, I can't stress the importance of the next 24 hours not just for us but the wider international community. So if you have to bunk up for one night...'

'Bunk up! Are we seven years old? Unless you mean hook up...'

'Shauna, you're getting giddy. What was in your tea?' Andy said whilst shaking his finger at her. Brian began to giggle, not a characteristic that any of us associated with him. Perhaps it was a sense of relief after his ordeal. It began as more of a snigger and then developed into a full chortle, the final straw being a loud snort as Brian lost control. Initially, there was silence. Berni politely bit her lip, Andy gave a little frown, and Jasmine looked startled, I was just surprised, but Shauna, well she was Shauna. The snort sent her off balance, she looked around for support before bursting out laughing and whacking Lacey on the arm. And then the whole group joined in, even Cagney who came inside to see what the hullabaloo was about. Everyone was laughing. And this was how the day ended, in a stone cottage in Grindleford, the night before one of the most dangerous and exciting days of our lives. Our group bonded through laughter just as we had at the very beginning when we had first entered the *Watcher 22* program. Tomorrow would be a very big day.

Who Knows What Tomorrow Brings?

Joe Cocker and Jennifer Warnes.

Who knows what tomorrow brings
In a world, few hearts survive
All I know, is the way I feel
When its real, I keep my pray alive

44

Chapter

Sleeping in bunk beds may sound fun, but it's probably better if you are a youngster and stress-free. Berni was a gentle snorer, Shauna, as expected, was a restless sleeper and Jasmine appeared to make no sound at all, which suggested she had been awake all night. I fell asleep, eventually, dreaming about Velociraptors swooping down on us while we tried to eat our afternoon tea. The most disturbing element of my dream/nightmare focused on Brown who was standing behind Shauna and was laughing at her, a mechanical unkind laugh. In my dream, I looked across at him, surprised by his merciless behaviour. Brown's eyes were dead, stony black and unblinking and he turned and pointed straight at me! I woke up with a start to the unwelcome coo-cooing of the wood pigeons. Perhaps that explained the appearance of the Velociraptors in my dream, that and the Museum visit, but not the evil version of Brown. I reached across for my Fit-bit watch. These days knowing the time was much more important than checking my step count. It's funny how priorities can change. It was quarter to seven. Being on the top bunk I had Shauna sleeping below me, she muttered and swore in her sleep, kicking the duvet from side to side in frustration. I looked across at Jasmine who was also on the top bunk. She was staring listlessly at the ceiling, I caught her eye and flashed her a reassuring smile, her expression remained the same. Maybe she slept with her eyes open. Berni continued to snore contentedly and I turned over as quietly as I could, hoping for an extra half an hour's rest. But the wood pigeons were relentless and in the background I could hear the sound of someone using the shower. Ten minutes later, just as I thought I might drift off and dream of Charlie, my poor neglected partner, Lacey banged on the door.

'Right you lot, rise and shine! We have work to do, people to see and places to go.' Shauna's response was no surprise to anyone who knew her. A stream of colourful expletives filled the air. Jasmine looked a little phased by it all, but Berni just shrugged her shoulders.

Within half an hour, we were all washed and dressed and sitting in the cosy kitchen sipping strong coffee and munching on white toast smothered in strawberry jam. This was no time for healthy eating. You could almost feel the tension crackling in the air. There was no lively banter here, not even from Shauna. Cagney retrieved Lacey from his lookout point and Jasmine set up a makeshift desk where she set up her laptop and began loading information from a USB stick. The briefcase was no longer attached to Jasmine's wrist. It now lay open and files and papers spilled out from it.

'What now? Not another bloody lesson? Surely not Cagney. For...'

Cagney was quite experienced at interrupting Shauna and didn't have the same soft spot for her that Lacey had.

'As you've asked so nicely Shauna, I'll give you the full introduction and I'll make it nice and long, just for you. Now move your chairs around so you can all see the screen.' Cagney was in no mood for high jinks today. 'Jasmine is a professor of Early Medieval History at the University of Manchester. She is an expert in her field and I would ask you all to listen to what she has to say. I know we have successfully found out the date, the time and the place for our big finale, but do we really know what we are looking for? Barry directed us to find Jasmine for a reason. So now we listen, even the smallest detail could be important. You all have paper and pens to write notes and any questions will be asked at the end. Is that clear?'

We all nodded our ascent and Jasmine began. She stood up without a moment's hesitation, her strong blue eyes scoured the group, demanding attention. She swung her long black hair over her left shoulder, brushed imaginary crumbs off her maroon corduroy pinafore and clicked on the presentation. All this while she was still facing us, a true professional. I just prayed that Shauna could control herself. The first slide came up and Jasmine began.

'Lindisfarne is also called Holy Island and approximately 160 people live there, but they do have 650,000 visitors every year. It's a tidal island off the North-east coast of England. Does everyone know what a tidal island is?'

Andy put his hand up and Shauna produced one of her mocking laughs. Jasmine turned to look at her and the steely blue stare did the trick.

'It's an island with one of those roads that can be submerged in seawater.'

'Good answer Andy, thank you.' Shauna silently mimicked Jasmine's words Andy just smiled and shook his head. Jasmine continued.

'You need to know about the tidal information as this restricts the times that we can cross, both on foot and by car. Lindisfarne is cut off from the mainland twice a day during high tide. During these times the causeway leading to the island is submerged, either in parts, or entirely, and it is impossible to cross.'

'So what you're saying is we could get stuck there or worse still be trapped on there with those Crytex scumbags?'

'I'm just saying that you need to know about the tides, Barry picked this location for a reason.' Shauna adopted one of her disgruntled expressions as Berni patted her arm reassuringly.

'I will continue. The island was originally home to a monastery, which was destroyed during the Viking invasions but then re-established as a priory following the Norman conquest of England.' Andy immediately shot his hand in up in the air. 'Yes, Andy?'

'1066.' he said, whilst giving a smug grin. It was too much for Shauna.

'Cocky bastard,'

Jasmine was not going to tolerate any more interruptions from Shauna. Before Cagney could jump in, Jasmine turned toward Shauna,

'If you can't be quiet, you'll have to leave. This information may prove to be very important and I won't allow you to distract everyone else. You can stay and listen or go, it's your choice.' Although Jasmine did not raise her voice, there was no mistaking her annoyance.

I could tell that Shauna was close to cracking, but we needed everyone in the team to participate. Lacey came to the rescue, as always.

'We need you to stay with us Shauna, just remember that it was your quick thinking that made the group question Barry's motives in the first place.'

As a rule, Shauna responded well to praise and that, combined with her fondness for Lacey, did the trick. She flashed Jasmine one of her looks, smirked at Andy and proceeded to scribble on her notepad, but more importantly, she remained seated which was a relief.

'I will continue. No more interruptions please, however heartfelt they may be.' she said as she looked across at both Andy and Shauna. That was a good move.

'Other notable sites built on the island are St. Mary the Virgin parish church, Lindisfarne castle and several lighthouses. In 2020, the island had three pubs, a hotel and a post office. The causeway is generally open from about three hours after high tide until two hours before the next high tide, but the period of closure can be extended during stormy weather. Despite these warnings, about one vehicle each month is stranded on the causeway. A sea rescue costs approximately £1,900, while an air rescue costs more than £4,000. The remote location and the complications which surround access may have been the reason that Barry chose it. When the moon is full and tide covers the causeway to the mainland, the ghost of St Cuthbert has been seen on the castle grounds.' Jasmine paused just as Berni raised her hand, even Shauna looked surprised.

'Yes Berni, what would you like to know?'

'When you mentioned the ghost of St Cuthbert, I felt something, it happens from time to time.' Jasmine looked suitably impressed.

'Could you tell us a little more Berni?'

'Spit it out Berni, for God's sake!' Berni sighed and gave Shauna a half smile.

'I don't see the ghost of St Cuthbert Jasmine. I know this will sound strange, but I can see the ghost of a white dog roaming some ruins. It's only a flash, a semblance of an image, I'll have more detail once we get there. These images are like previews triggered by words, once on site I will pick up more from the location.' Jasmine looked stunned and then began to slowly nod her head.

'I haven't seen it Berni, but legend has it that the ghost of a phantom white dog also roams the ruin and jumps out at people.'

'I just can't bloody wait to get there.' Shauna said and Berni simply shrugged her shoulders.

Who Let the Dogs Out

Baha Men

Who let the dogs out?
Who, who, who, who, who?

45

Three hours after Jasmine's briefing, we arrived in Alnwick in Northumberland and duly headed to the Hog's Head which was conveniently situated just by the busy A1. We were bundled off to another meeting room and seated around yet another meeting table. We were given refreshments and then the planning began for our trip to Lindisfarne. Lacey still reminded us that today was 23/10/2022 as if any of us had forgotten. By 10.11 pm we all need to have crossed the causeway and have found and solved find the final clue.

Jasmine sprang into action, she was very excited to be in such proximity to her beloved Holy Island. She told us all about Alnwick Castle and Shauna's ears pricked up when she mentioned that the castle was probably best known for the Harry Potter films and the TV series Downton Abbey.

'Lacey, can we go and visit the castle?' Shauna pleaded.

'Let's see Shauna, it's now 3.30 pm and we have to get to Lindisfarne before the tide turns, find the clue, decipher it, and then escape. We will most probably have been pinged by ANPR tracking and Crytex hunters will now be on our tail. So what do you think?' His voice increased in volume before he threw his pen across the table.

'Well seen as you've put it like that, you patronising b....'

'That will do Shauna.' uncharacteristically, it was Berni who snapped at Shauna. 'Lacey, could I ask what ANPR stands for? I'm not very good at acronyms.' Shauna didn't dare ask what an acronym was.

'It stands for Automatic Number Plate Recognition.' Cagney said, glancing across at Shauna.

'Ooh, I know where I've heard that before! It was on the TV, that programme Hunted where ordinary people go on the run from a team of hunters.'

'Well that's as maybe, but do you understand what the ANPR can do?' he didn't wait for an answer. 'Police ANPR cameras are located on main roads and motorways. They take a photograph of every vehicle license plate which passes them. The technology reads the vehicle registration plates and creates location data. If Crytex has hacked into the police ANPR, and it will have, we will have been tracked, which is why we need to get back on the road.' Lacey had been hard at work setting up a 24-hour timetable on the whiteboard. It included the tide times, our ETA, the location of the safe house and details about our backup detail both on the ground and in the air.

Within twenty minutes we had been fed and watered and we were back on the road. There were now unmarked police cars accompanying us and a helicopter was flying overhead. The flashing blue lights had been attached to the front of both Range Rovers and we were now positioned within a protective convoy. I have no idea what speed we were travelling at, but it was significantly faster than the speed limit. We were, of course, all wearing seat belts. You could feel the tension in the air. No one spoke, not even Shauna, the only sound was the constant chatter of the walkie-talkies.

It was an uneventful journey and thirty minutes later we started to see the signs for Lindisfarne. It was now 4.45 pm. Ominous clouds loomed over the choppy sea and the light dwindled. And then we saw it, the raised road, the causeway. It cut through the wet sands, this was our passage to Holy Island. Within hours it would be completely submerged and in-passable. A bright yellow warning sign pointed out the dangers, advising people not to cross when 'the water reached the causeway'. It is hard to believe that people take such risks making this crossing, but as Jasmine pointed out, one vehicle a month gets stranded. At last, there was a feeling of excitement in the Range Rover and as expected it was Shauna who broke the silence.

'How cool is this? Jasmine, does this road get completely covered when the tide comes in?' Shauna asked politely.

'Yes, it will be completely submerged from midnight tonight until 5 a.m.'

'So we're bloody mooned there until dawn? Is that what you're saying?' Jasmine looked a little confused, she was unused to Shauna's occasional literary hiccup. I was just glad that Andy and Cagney were travelling in the other Range Rover or they would have been giggling by now. Berni leaned across to Shauna and put her straight. Fortunately, she took it well and even rephrased the question.

245

'I meant to ask if we will be marooned on Holy Island for five hours?'

'We will Shauna. That's exactly right.'

'Fuckin' cool!'

Lacey looked back at me from the front mirror and raised his eyebrows as I shook my head. Trying to tone down Shauna's colourful language was a lost cause. Driving across the sand-covered road, which would soon be submerged in the sea, was a great experience. Everyone enjoyed the ride, cutting through the dunes on this magical causeway. The views of the Northumberland coast were stunning. We then headed inland and came to a stop at Chare Ends car park. The mood had lifted and we were ready for the next adventure. There was no time for chatting, Cagney and Lacey grabbed their laptop bags from the boot and we were marched double time passed the quaint hotel and gift shops. Within minutes we arrived at Curlew Cottage, a pretty stone cottage that proved to be deceptively large once inside.

A wood-burning stove heats the large sitting room and the table is set for tea, complete with scones and cups and saucers in place. Shauna, Andy and Berni flopped down on the large corner sofa and I relaxed into a cosy armchair. Jasmine followed Cagney and Lacey into the kitchen.

'Stick the kettle on while you're in there!' Shauna said, flashing a cheeky grin.

'Get your lazy...'

'Lazy what Cagney?'

Cagney coughed. 'Get in here Shauna and do it yourself, we have other priorities at the moment.'

246

'It's OK, I can do it.'

'Thank you, Jasmine.'

'Helena can you draw the curtains, it's dark now and people may be able to see in from the street. I duly obliged and just as I was pulling the curtains together, that's when I saw him. There was no mistake, it was definitely him. Before I could alert the others there was a loud rat-a-tat-tat on the front door and everyone went quiet.

Let 'Em In

Paul McCartney

Someone's knockin' at the door
Somebody's ringin' the bell
Someone's knockin' at the door
Somebody's ringin' the bell
Do me a favor
Open the door and let 'em in

46

Chapter

When you know that Crytex hunters are chasing you, it heightens awareness. After all, we are just normal civilians, not Special Agents. The knock on the door instilled fear, everyone froze and no one went to answer the door. Cagney did spring into action, he loaded his firearm and went towards the door. Lacey signalled for us all to lie low, even Shauna obeyed.

'It's only Brown.' I told Lacey as he pushed my head behind a cushion. 'Surely he's not that dangerous. Don't shoot him, Cagney!'

'We should have had a warning message from HQ about this. Did you get anything, Lacey? How do we proceed?'

'Get Brown in off the street Cagney.' he wrenched open the door and pulled Brown into the room.

'Before you do anything or say anything you might regret, I have papers. I have been cleared by MI5.' Lacey was in contact with HQ, frantically trying to get answers. Cagney pushed Brown into the dining area. It was hardly a surprise who broke the silence first.

'Jesus! What are you doing here you fuckin' snake? Haven't you done enough damage?'

'We don't know the full story, Shauna, so button it.' Andy said firmly.

'There's a lot we don't know about, it's better to keep an open mind.' Brian added. Cagney searched Brown thoroughly, he did not have a phone with him but he wasn't wearing a wire. Lacey then forced him to sit down on one of the kitchen chairs and the paperwork was snatched from his hand.

'He has got the all clear.' Cagney's voice was loud enough for us all to hear.

'If I could just explain.' he said, looking round at us all.

'You've got five minutes and then we move on.'

'I know you all think I'm a traitor.' he looked at each of us in turn and then stopped when his eyes fell on Jasmine. 'Lacey before I bare my soul, could you introduce me to the new group member?'

'That's Jasmine. She's new, from the University, an expert on Lindisfarne, and here to help. That's all you need to know. Now get on with it.'

Brown hesitated. 'Very well, if Jasmine has made it through clearance…'

'You cheeky f…'

'Quiet Shauna! Let the man speak.' Cagney said what we were all thinking.

Brown then stood up to deliver his news, he was adept at public speaking. 'In a nutshell, Crytex kidnapped my sister and my young nephew, and if I refused to comply they threatened to torture them both. The recordings would then be released on the dark web.' Brown paused. 'Before you judge me, you have to understand that I had no choice. Ask yourselves if you would you like your sister and young nephew to be in a room with Maxim

249

and Lars?' Brown looked around at the group. Brian was close to tears, the memories were still fresh for him. 'As if the threat wasn't enough of an incentive to make me conform, the photographs of them tied up were unbearable. I repeat I had no choice.' Brian visibly shuddered before nodding his head in agreement. 'I had to leak sensitive information and for that, I am sorry as I put you and your families at risk.'

'What do you mean? We knew that you'd put us in danger, but not our families as well! Is Charlie and everyone else's family OK?' Everyone looked at me, it wasn't often that I raised my voice, I even beat Shauna to it.

'I'll take over now Brown.' Cagney said as he pushed Brown onto one of the chairs. 'Look you can't judge him. Would you let your family be tortured by those nut jobs? I think not. And to answer your question Helena all your families are being protected and have been relocated.'

'Thank God. It's bad enough putting ourselves on the front line, but not our families, they have no part in this.'

'Well actually we all have a part in this Andy, but please be assured all your families are now safe.'

'Could I ask how you resolved the Brown family kidnapping issue? I understand if you are unable to tell us.'

'I can only tell you a shortened version Berni as that's all I have.' Cagney paused as we all gave nods of understanding. 'The CIA used satellite tracking to locate Brown's sister and nephew. Fortunately, the Crytex agents had slipped up and their cover was broken. Jenni and Carl were involved in the rescue and all of them are safe.' Cagney paused. 'However, we are now at risk, if we have been tracked it's only a matter of time before the Crytex hunters find us. We need to plan our next move very carefully. There is one more thing that Brown needs to explain to you all.'

'Indeed. If you cast your mind back to the very start, to the reading of Barry's will, I was given a separate envelope which I read in another room. Do you remember?'

There was a collective nod. Poor Jasmine just looked dazed. 'Barry cleverly decided to keep specific details about the final location a secret that only I knew and I have not told a soul.'

'Perhaps you haven't noticed Brown, we are in the final location, so what the…'

'Do you know exactly where the final clue is? No, you do not. This is a small island, but we need to use our limited time efficiently.

'He's right.' Jasmine said unexpectedly. 'We need some direction about the location and time to decode the clue.

'She's right. Our focus has been on gathering the clues moving locations and trying to stay safe. But what do we actually know about the grand finale?'

'We have focused on getting here on the right day and at the right time. We have a code we need to use to destroy *Watcher 22*, but we don't know how we are meant to do it.'

'And Barry the bastard did! Worst still he gave the final piece of the jigsaw to Brown.' Shauna looked daggers at him. 'What I'd like to know is what Cagney and Lacey thought we were going to do next. If Brown hadn't shown up…'

'We do have intelligence, Shauna.' Lacey said defensively. 'And Brown's letter just confirms what we already knew.'

'That's not really true is it Lacey?' Berni said gently. 'Not that it matters, but it is always better to be straight with us.'

'We don't have time for this.' Brown said impatiently. 'We can de-brief later. Right now we need to work out the best way to finish this. Barry has hidden something in the church...'

'St Mary the Virgin church to be exact.'

'Thank you, Jasmine.' Cagney took a breath.'Barry has hidden something in St Mary the Virgin church and it's approximately ten minutes away on foot.'

'Although we would like to believe that Crytex does not know the final destination, they will likely go for the top three places on the island. It's doubtful that they have sleeper agents here on Lindisfarne, but they may have eyes on the ground here or satellite feed. Only a fool would underestimate them.'

'Let's hope the buggers mistime it and they all drown!'

'Thank you, Shauna. I think we also need to assume that Maxim and Lars will be with them. Now it's over to Jasmine who will brief you on Brown's notes.'

'Although we know the correct location, once there we will need to find the parchment, break the code using the key supplied by Brown and then regroup. When we do regroup every team member must be present to log in to *Watcher 22* and delete it forever.'

'Jesus! Not too much pressure on us then!'

'Now to pick the teams.' Before the process could begin, both radio earpieces relayed messages simultaneously. Cagney relayed the news,

'Two Crytex hunter vehicles are crossing the causeway. We need to move.'

Born To Run

Bruce Springsteen

Oh honey, tramps like us
Baby, we were born to run
Come on with me, tramps like us
Baby, we were born to run

47

Chapter

Night fell quickly on the island and suddenly everything seemed much more intense. The time had come to split into two groups, which would hopefully divide the hunters. Crytex could have people on the island watching the group, it would be a huge mistake to underestimate them.

'Right, there's no time to lose. The Crytex hunters will be on the island in approximately thirty minutes. We need to move and quickly. Lacey, sort the groups out while I check the laptop.' Cagney unzipped the laptop bag and logged into the network.

'Is it going to be like being picked for the netball team at school? I bloody hated it.'

'Please be quiet Shauna. Let me think.'

'How many locations do we need to cover Lacey, let's start with that.'

'You're right Helena, we have decided to use three locations to try and confuse the hunters. I think that Jasmine, Berni, Brown and Cagney should go to the church and find the parchment. They can start decoding and Cagney is armed, so he can protect them. Brown will go back to the car park and get the Range Rover. Once this group has the code, Brown will drive them to the harbour. The rest of us will be on foot, with torches. The decoy group will have two sub-teams. Shauna and I will head straight for the castle, anyone following us on foot should take the bait.

'What! Are we being sacrificed for the greater good, just to be picked off? Bloody typical.'

'Calm down Shauna. If the decoy groups can draw the hunters away it gives the other larger group more time to decode the final clue. If Helena and Andy have both been seen by Lars and Maxim, the hunters should then go to the Crown and Anchor pub which is just down the road here, no complaining Shauna. The local shops will all be closed now. Helena, you tell the innkeeper that you are staying at St Oswald's cottage, and that will lay a trail of breadcrumbs for the hunters. Order drinks then leave by the back door and head passed the cottage and proceed to the harbour. As the castle will be closed, Shauna and I will circumvent it and head for the harbour as well.'

'Just so you know Lacey, you won't be doing any circumventing with me!'

It was Berni who giggled first, then Andy, and then me, even Jasmine smiled. Surprisingly the loud guffawing came from Cagney, who tried to disguise it from behind the laptop. By this time even Lacey was chuckling. It was just what we needed.

Once things had calmed down, Lacey finished the briefing and gave us all torches and plastic wallets containing a map of the different destinations.

'When we all regroup with the clues decoded, the team will access the *Watcher 22* program and eradicate it for good.'

'And our escape Lacey?' How do we get away from here?'

'That's a good question Berni, we will be picked up by boats and home we go.'

'And the Crytex scum? What happens to them?'

'We are heading to the harbour for a reason and not just to get our ride home. It's remote. The Crytex agents will be taken care of and there are two in particular that deserve a beating.'

'That's all we can say. It's dangerous to share any more information, just in case one of us gets captured.'

'That's a reassuring note to end on. Thanks a bunch, Lacey.'

'Shauna stop your yapping. We leave first and head for the castle. Next Jasmine, Berni, Brown and Cagney will go to the church, leaving via the back door. Helena and Andy will go last and lock up the cottage, head for the Crown and Anchor and you know the rest. Good luck teams, see you all at the harbour. And make sure no one follows you there! This is extremely important and remember that all team leaders need to be there.'

Andy and I were the last to leave. Once Curlew cottage was locked up, we headed for the pub. It wasn't too difficult to get a conversation going with the landlady and talk about St Oswald's cottage and pretend we were staying there for the night. We did treat ourselves to a very swift drink and just as we'd ordered the second, Maggie, the pub landlady almost threw a spanner in the works.

'David is normally in about now.' she said whilst checking her watch. 'You will have already met him though, you know the owner of St Oswald's cottage. He likes a drink does David.'

Andy was quick to respond, 'We only saw him for a few moments, Maggie, just checking in and that. We'd be happy to put a drink behind the bar for him unless he drinks Champagne of course.'

'That's good of you. But you can give it to him yourselves shortly.' she said as she winked and she put our drinks on the bar. Andy paid and then asked if we could pop out to the back for a cigarette.

'Your drinks will be fine on the bar. Just go through the snug, there's a shelter out the back that the smokers use.' Andy thanked her and we headed outside, whether Maggie was just being friendly or giving us a warning was unclear, either way, we had to leave. We cut past the smoker's hut and back onto the main road. It was only a short walk to St Oswald's cottage. We were checking to see if we'd been followed, but there was no one behind us. So far so good. Just as we were walking passed the cottage, the door opened and a well-built chap came up the path and he was whistling to himself.

'Evening.' he said and gave us a nod. We both said good evening as Dave was eager to get to the pub.

'That's how it is in these small places, everyone knows everyone. If Crytex get to the pub they'll ask out about us and head for St Oswald's cottage. Remember Dave and Maggie don't know our final destination. But we may have blown our cover using St Oswald's cottage as a decoy location.

'We did what we could Andy. Now we head for the harbour.'

Shauna and Lacey were on their way to the castle. It was a fifteen-minute walk and although a few cars passed them on the road, so far no one had stopped them or followed them.

'Do you think we'll get all the timings right Lacey?'

'I hope so Shauna. It will depend on how the other team goes about finding the clue. Once we have that and combine it with the XA31 blackout code we got from the Royal Exchange theatre, then we will know.'

'How dangerous are the Crytex scumbags Lacey? Brian is still traumatised by his kidnapping.'

'They are brutal Shauna. Our weak spot is the team at the church as they will have the codes and if Crytex gets hold of them there's no saying what will happen.'

'Jesus Lacey, you know how to cheer a girl up!'

'That's as maybe, but what do you think of Lindisfarne Castle?' Shauna gasped. They were so lucky that it was a full moon.

'It is no wonder that this castle is one of the most photographed castles in England. It was a fort and that's why it's perched on the top of the hill. What a wonderful castle in such an amazing place looking out over the sea. What do you think Shauna?'

'It's fuckin' impressive, I can't lie! It reminds me of a walnut whip.' Lacey started laughing. 'A walnut whip castle, just brilliant.'

'It's a shame we can't go in it. The hunters will know it's closed.'

'But for all they know, the final clue could be hidden in the walls. I love the turrets and the way the stone walls curve around it.' Lacey was taken with the castle which was bathed in the moonlight. The moment was interrupted by a message through his earpiece.

'No more time for sightseeing. Helena and Andy are at the harbour we need to move on.'

'Farewell walnut whip castle, for now at least.'

Castle on the Hill

Ed Sheeran

I'm on my way
Driving at 90 down those country lanes
Singing to Tiny Dancer
And I miss the way you make me feel, and it's real
When we watched the sunset over the castle on the hill

48

Chapter

Jasmine, Berni and Cagney made their way to St Mary the Virgin Church. Cagney followed a few paces behind as he was on high alert. The full Watcher team and the code needed to make it to the harbour. They had thirty minutes head start over Crytex and every minute was going to count. After making good time, they arrived at Lindisfarne Priory which was founded in the 7th century and preceded the church which was built much later. The mix of moonlight and torchlight on the extensive ruins was simply spectacular. The magnificent rainbow arch was the most famous feature of the Priory. A soaring, elegant reminder of the beautiful medieval building that was once there.

Berni shuddered as they approached the Priory. She hadn't realised that the Priory and the church were so close together. Beautiful as the ruins were, with their lovely archways and columns, Berni could not feel the peaceful ambiance of the religious order who once resided there.

'Can we move on, please? We need to find the last clue and return to the others.' 'All OK Berni?' Cagney asked as he led the team into the church. Berni just shrugged. Fortunately, she became distracted by the beautiful stained glass windows and stone arches, which looked magnificent by the candlelight.

'Get your torches on now please.' Brown handed Jasmine Barry's letter that he had received at the will reading and she dutifully read it aloud.

'The grand finale will be at Lindisfarne. The clue will be hidden at St Mary the Virgin Church, check the pews and work quickly. I am sure that Crytex will be close behind you. I feel sure that you will have set up a decoy team, perhaps more than one, and sent them to other locations to throw Crytex off the scent. Godspeed. Destroy *Watcher 22* for the greater good. Its power is unbelievable and the potential is terrifying. Jasmine, I say this to you, 'All have sinned and fall short of God's glory...' Our team will win and it will finally be over. Tell Berni she was right. Regards, the black sheep Barry.'

'I've no idea why I was right or about what. Let's move on, Jasmine do you have the reference?' Berni was keen to get out of the Priory.

'Yes. It's from the Bible, Romans 3, and very apt after what you have all told me.'

'Let's move. Jasmine follow the clue and search one end of pew 3 and Berni on the other end. I'll be keeping a close lookout.'

Ten minutes later after flicking through prayer books and running their fingers under the prayer book shelf, they found nothing.

'It's time to go under.' Berni said as she pulled out one of the prayer kneeling cushions. Jasmine did the same and they slowly worked their way along the pew.

'I've got it!' Jasmine was lying flat and had positioned her torch carefully. 'It was taped under the pew with masking tape. I guess nobody ever crawls under here.' Berni called Cagney in for the grand opening, this is what all their adventures had led them to.

'OK, read it quickly. The Crytex hunters are parking up at Chare Ends car park. We need to move and now!' Jasmine unfurled the parchment 'It's in Latin, it will just take a few moments to translate.' Brown scanned the message which read: Index *Watcher 22*. Formam circuli. Andy coniungere est. Tenere manus. Omnes hunc codicem visualise: <<<WR22h.exit ( ) Intra eum. Deinde imposuisti XA31. Post niger, reboot et recenseo.

Cagney put his hand to his earpiece. 'Translate it later. We move and now!'

They came out of the church and entered the ruins of the priory and that was when Berni froze. She was fixed to the spot, absolutely terrified. Right in front of her, she could see the phantom white dog that roams the priory at night.

'Do you see it? Can't you see the white hound? It's snarling and ready to pounce.'

'It's not really here Berni.' Cagney said gently. 'It's a ghost, remember?'

Berni was not convinced. Jasmine took Berni's hand and Brown grabbed her other hand, together they manoeuvred her away from the Priory and the phantom dog that only she could see. Berni was still shaking. But with the combination of the salty sea air and the team's reassurance, she began to rally.

Ten minutes later they arrived at the harbour. Lacey guided the group to one of the huts, which was a boat conversion. There were several upturned herring boats, which now served as storage huts. Lacey had found an empty one and at last, the team was reunited. Cagney debriefed the group, whilst Jasmine quickly translated the message. Shauna and I comforted Berni. Lacey had produced a most welcome flask of whisky from his jacket pocket which helped. He was now on guard outside the boat hut. Cagney was setting up the laptop attaching it to a Portable Laptop Power Bank, as there was no power in the hut. Fortunately, Lindisfarne has fast fibre internet and Cagney easily connected to Wi-Fi.

'I will now read the message that Jasmine translated. Here goes.

Upload *Watcher 22*. Form a circle. Andy must connect. Hold hands. Everyone visualise this code: <<<WR22h.exit ( ) Enter it. Then upload XA31. After the blackout, reboot and review.'

It seemed short and sweet, but we all knew from the past, that things are not always what they seem. Cagney called Lacey to the hut and informed him about the next stage as he loaded *Watcher 22*, the original Watcher team formed a circle. And this time we could all hear the music.

The Final Countdown

Europe

We're leavin' together
But still it's farewell
And maybe we'll come back
To Earth, who can tell?
I guess there is no one to blame
We're leaving ground (leaving ground)
Will things
ever be the same again?

It's the final countdown
The final countdown

49

Watcher 22 was up and running. We were just waiting to get full access. Brown was logging in, as he had worked for Experenta *XP*. It was fairly cramped in the hut, but we managed to form a circle, albeit from a seated position and we held hands as instructed. It wasn't long before Shauna had something to say.

'I hope you lot don't get blasted back into my dodgy past.'

'So do we Shauna, I bet it's messy.' Andy answered, digging her gently in the ribs.

'I don't think my heart could take it.' I said and looked across at Shauna.

Jasmine had written the code in large block capitals on a piece of card. She stood to one side, she was not part of the circle.

'How will it know it's us and our group?'

'Funny you should ask.' Cagney said.'Jasmine if you would give Andy the glasses.' Jasmine produced a fancy pair of AI algorithm glasses and handed them to Andy. 'I've already scanned the QR code which connects you to Wi-Fi and the *Watcher 22* program. I could feel

Andy's grip tighten. Andy put the glasses on and I could feel his body jolt as he entered the program.

'Everyone look at the code and visualise it.' Jasmine held up the piece of card which had the code 'WR22h. exit' written on it.

'Shauna please concentrate.'

Shauna mimicked Jasmine. Berni glared at her and she quietened down. There was the familiar crackling sound as Andy entered the program. His body began to shudder. This was a place none of us wanted to go.

'Cagney enter the code. Andy is struggling!'

'I'm waiting for the green light.'

'Get a move on in there!' Lacey shouted through the doorway. 'Crytex are en route, they must have worked out our exit.'

'Quiet Lacey! Everyone focus.'

Andy began to mutter incoherently. *Watcher 22* was designed to simulate live flashbacks and Andy was unprepared. I focused on the code and we all began to chant it.

'WR22h.exit'

I hoped this would remind Andy that we were all with him.

'Green-light! Cagney shouted and entered the code into the computer. Next, he loaded the code for XA31.

Andy went limp, the force between us was broken. Had we done enough?

'Are you alright Andy?' Berni asked as Andy slumped back into the chair. Andy took a deep breath before answering. 'I'm Ok Berni. *Watcher 22* flashed me back, right back to when I was a child and then the strangest thing happened. A woman appeared, I didn't know her.

She reached out her hand and stroked my hair and reassured me, she just kept saying that everything would be alright and to hold on. And then the weirdest thing happened, Helena's psycho Guide, Flint, aka Alan Rickman, burst into my head. Flint told her to let me go. He just kept telling her to let me go. There was no time to unpick Andy's message. I was secretly delighted that Flint was still around, especially as in our world he has sadly passed away.

'The blackout has happened Cagney!' The laptop screen had gone black and all the lights on the island were now out.

'Look! I can see the lights of the rib, it's heading towards the jetty. Everyone move! Grab all your things. Shit, there are the car lights of the Crytex hunters coming this way! Move it!'

We headed for the jetty. The rib was approaching at speed. This would be close. Soon the hunters would be on foot. We got to the end of the jetty, just as the rib arrived.

'Everyone on board.' Lacey said as he helped Berni down the stone steps and onto the rib. Cagney was first aboard and helped each one of us. The stone steps were slippy and the rib was moving to the rhythm of the sea.

Once we were all boarded and strapped in, we headed out to sea and the rib picked up speed. We had finally done it! Escaped from the island and the Crytex hunters. Everyone cheered! Thank God! Then came the deafening sound. Two Army Wildcat Mk1 helicopters were flying low and approaching the jetty, The rotational relative wind from the rotor blades could be felt in the air and on the sea. The helicopters hovered over the jetty and ropes were dropped down allowing the troops to deploy. The Crytex hunters had, at last, met their match. The rib slowed, there was no urgency now. Andy rebooted the laptop and accessed the program.

'We did it! *Watcher 22* is no more.' he shouted and we all cheered. 'Well done. It is finally over.'

'Thank fuck for that!' Shauna said jubilantly. 'Next time I go for counselling I will insist on it being a human being. No more interactive IT counselling for me.'

We were all allowed this moment of glory. The relief spread through us all. Barry had started us off on this adventure with his Six Keys and now we had completed the mission and could go home.

'I would just like to say one thing. You can release your harnesses for a moment, but don't stand up.' The rib had now slowed right down. We released the safety straps and turned to face Berni. 'I think I have worked out who Margaret is. The lady that spoke to Andy. I may be mistaken but...'

'For fuck's sake Berni just tell us!

'It's Barry's wife.'

What! Is she alive? Did he save her? Or is she stuck in *Watcher 22*?'

'I feel her presence and I think she is on Lindisfarne, which is why Barry brought us here. I suddenly felt cold. And then I made the connection. Barry was a clever bastard alright and a good liar.

'I think I know what happened Berni. I think Barry exchanged his life for hers. I don't pretend to understand it all. But I do know he loved her and she died prematurely in a car accident. The cost of saving her took its toll and that's why he died of a heart attack. Her name is Margaret, but that's often shortened to Maggie.' I paused waiting for Andy to make the connection.

'You mean Maggie, as in Maggie the landlady at the Crown and Anchor pub, the lady that served us?'

'Yes Andy, I think that was her, what a remote place to hide and remain unseen. Crytex doesn't know about her…'

'And neither do Experenta *XP*.'

'And they never will Brown, do you hear me! Never!'

'After this experience Shauna, having my family kidnapped and being rescued by a rib and watching troops descend from a helicopter, after this experience, Barry's secret is safe with me. After all, he gave his life for it.'

'And don't you forget it, Brown! All our lives depend on it remaining a secret.'

'And it will. Do we all promise?'

We managed to hold hands, this time with Jasmine, Cagney and Lacey included and we all swore a solemn oath.

The rib began to power up its engines and head back into the night. And then you could just hear it, the music, and then it got louder. Now everyone could hear it and everyone joined in.

We Are the Champions

Queen

We are the champions, my friends
And we'll keep on fighting till the end
We are the champions
We are the champions
No time for losers
'Cause we are the champions of the World

Acknowledgements

I would like to thank my partner Graham Frost, my trusty wingman, for his support with the storyline and the wonderful photographs. I am also grateful to my lovely daughters; Sarah for her unfailing enthusiasm and confidence in my writing and Emma for her continuous positivity and Instagram wizardry.

A big thank you also to my mum and sister Judith for their continued encouragement and backing

Thank you also to my brilliant beta-readers, Graham Frost, Michele Parks and SandraC for their eagle-eyed proofreading and advice.

I also want to thank my lovely writing buddies, The Dissectologists: Suzanne, Flo, Annemarie, Jane, Michelle, Louise, Lisa, Kate and Deborah who have given me reassurance and boosted my confidence throughout. Special thanks also to Michelle and Suzanne for all their creative advice on the cover design.

Hats off to the enthusiastic and indomitable Michael Heppell, Sunday Times best-selling author and *Write That Book Masterclass,* his advice and motivation pushed me out of my comfort zone and into the world of social media.

Many thanks to my loyal readers who have followed me and supported me throughout.

A final big thank you to Grosvenor House Publishing Company for your dedication and expertise.

About the Author

When I was six years old my primary school teacher asked the class what they wanted to be when they were grown-ups. I wrote down author which I spelt Orthor. Life got in the way, but I continued to write poems and had some articles published in the local newspaper. After working in a bank and a building society, I knew the world of business was not for me and returned to education. I have a degree in English and Creative writing and Post Graduate qualifications in Education and Specialist Teaching.

I wrote and published my first book *The Leavings* in 2014, followed by *Watcher 22* in 2019. *Six Keys* is the final book in the trilogy. All of my books are stand alone and contain very different stories, but have the same characters. I have loved writing all my books and I already have ideas for the next one!

If you like my books please leave a review on Amazon or contact me on the platforms below.

Facebook: https://www.facebook.com/sue.collinge.5
Instagram: @slc.books

Six Keys Playlist

1. *One Voice* - Barry Manilow
2. *Paint It, Black* - The Rolling Stones
3. *Absolute Beginners* - David Bowie
4. *I'm still standing* - Elton John
5. *Red light spells danger* - Billy Ocean
6. *Under pressure* - Queen and David Bowie
7. *One night only* - Jennifer Hudson
8. *Jailhouse Rock* - Elvis Presley
9. *Danger Zone* - Kenny Loggins
10. *I've Gotta Get a Message to You* - Bee Gees
11. *Watching the Detectives* - Elvis Costello
12. *Runaway baby* - Bruno Mars
13. *Somebody's Watching Me* - Rockwell
14. *Sweet Child O' Mine* - Guns N' Roses
15. *No one* - Alicia Keys
16. *If I could turn back time* - Cher
17. *Good Things Come To Those Who Wait* - Nathan Sykes
18. *Miss You Like Crazy* - Natalie Cole
19. *Pompeii* - Bastille
20. *Chain reaction* - Diana Ross
21. *Boulevard of Broken Dreams* - Green Day
22. *Witchcraft* - Frank Sinatra

23. *Run for home* - Lindisfarne
24. *Hallelujah* - Celine Dion & The Canadian Tenors
25. *Brave* - Sarah Bareilles
26. *Stand By Me* - Ben E King
27. *Help me make it through the night* - Sammi Smith
28. *I've Gotta Get a Message to You* - Bee Gees
29. *Something inside so strong* - Labi Siffre
30. *Drop the Pilot* - Joan Armatrading
31. *Eye of the tiger* - Survivor
32. *I can see clearly* - Johnny Nash
33. *Don't Stop Believin'* – Journey
34. *Runaway Baby* - Bruno Mars
35. *Livin' on a prayer* - Bon Jovi
36. *So Good to See You* - Cheap Trick
37. *Firework* - Katy Perry
38. *Picture this* - Blondie
39. *The Climb* - Joe McElderry
40. *Midnight Train to Georgia* - Gladys Knight & the Pips
41. *I'm still standin'* - Elton John
42. *Where the Streets Have No Name* - U2
43. *Who Knows What Tomorrow Brings?* - Joe Cocker and Jennifer Warnes.
44. *Who Let the Dogs Out* - Baha Men
45. *Let 'Em In* - Paul McCartney
46. *Born To Run* - Bruce Springsteen
47. *Castle on the Hill* - Ed Sheeran
48. *The Final Countdown* - Europe
49. *We Are the Champions* - Queen